RANCH
ROGUES

WESTERN *Lovers*™

LINDSAY McKENNA

CHASE THE CLOUDS

Published by Silhouette Books
America's Publisher of Contemporary Romance

If you purchased this book without a cover you should be aware that this book is stolen property. It was reported as "unsold and destroyed" to the publisher, and neither the author nor the publisher has received any payment for this "stripped book."

To Nancy Csonka and Joan Schwartz,
fellow horsewomen, who share my love
of a good horse, the outdoors and
our friendship

SILHOUETTE BOOKS
300 East 42nd St.,
New York, N.Y. 10017

ISBN 0-373-88503-2

CHASE THE CLOUDS

Copyright © 1983 by Lindsay McKenna

All rights reserved. Except for use in any review, the reproduction or utilization of this work in whole or in part in any form by any electronic, mechanical or other means, now known or hereafter invented, including xerography, photocopying and recording, or in any information storage or retrieval system, is forbidden without the written permission of the editorial office, Silhouette Books, 300 East 42nd Street, New York, NY 10017 U.S.A.

All characters in this book have no existence outside the imagination of the author and have no relation whatsoever to anyone bearing the same name or names. They are not even distantly inspired by any individual known or unknown to the author, and all incidents are pure invention.

This edition published by arrangement with Harlequin Enterprises B.V.

® and TM are trademarks of Harlequin Enterprises B.V., used under license. Trademarks indicated with ® are registered in the United States Patent and Trademark Office, the Canadian Trade Marks Office and in other countries.

Printed in U.S.A.

One

"Mrs. Daguerre, I can assure you I'm not used to having people fall short of their obligations to me. Especially ones where a legal contract is signed and services are promised."

Danielle stiffened in her chair and stared across the small office that was located within the main stabling barn. She was tall for a horse trainer, almost five foot nine, but she felt diminutive against the man who stood in the doorway blocking the afternoon April sun that slanted across his broad shoulders. Easing out of the black leather desk chair, she folded her arms against her small breasts, feeling positively threatened by his detached coolness. His eyes, the shade of pewter gray, assessed her with mild interest.

"Mr. Reese," she began, taking a firm tone that she would normally use with misbehaving horses, "my ex-husband signed that document over a year ago to ride your three-day-event thoroughbred, I didn't."

He gave her a thin, cutting smile, one corner of his generous mouth pulling upward. Removing the Stetson from his rich, dark hair, he let the hat dangle in his right hand. "Right now I don't care who signed it. I'm sorry that your marriage was broken up, but an agreement is an agreement."

"Your stallion, Altair, has a nasty name on the show circuit," she reminded him stubbornly. As much as she hated to use her ex-husband's name, she went on, "Jean's notes tell me that he's shy of water jumps, headstrong and impulsive and won't listen to his rider."

His cool, twisted smile remained as he studied her across the distance. "Yes, I'm afraid he's a bit like me in some respects—hard to handle."

Dany's nostrils flared with a show of contempt. Pointing at the fact sheets compiled on the jumper, she said, "You can't take a range horse and make him a Grand Prix jumper, Mr. Reese. It just can't be done. Your stallion has been mishandled too long, and I don't have the time or inclination to try and retrain him for you, contract or no contract."

His gray eyes glittered with an unnamed emotion. "Altair was out of the finest thoroughbred stock money can buy, Mrs. Daguerre. The fact that his dam was stolen and then abandoned in the middle of the Nevada desert with Altair at her side has no bearing on his abilities. It's true he was raised in the wild with a herd of mustangs. He was caught as a four-year-old by wranglers who busted him for use as a cow horse." He shrugged his broad shoulders. "I saw him by accident when I was looking over a herd of charlois, and bought him immediately."

Dany tried to quell her frustration. "It's a very touching story, Mr. Reese but—"

"You haven't heard all of it," he ground out softly.

Something in the tone of his voice warned her to remain motionless. "All right," she capitulated, "tell me the rest of it. But it won't change my mind."

"The more facts you have, the better you'll be able to weigh your decision," he parried.

"I'm waiting...."

"The wrangler who owned him tried to beat the spirit out of Altair. Consequently, he's pretty scarred up from it, both physically and emotionally. I knew he was thoroughbred by his conformation. When the owner showed me the mare, her tattoo number was stamped on the inside of her upper lip. All I had to do was call the registry and confirm Altair's breeding. He can't be registered, but in Grand Prix, papers don't mean a thing. Ability does.''

"I suppose it doesn't mean a thing that he's a range horse?''

Sam Reese gave her an odd smile. "You can come from the wrong side of the tracks and still make it. I'm sure you're familiar with Nautilus, the palomino gelding they found at some riding stable?''

Dany nodded. "Yes, a rags-to-riches story of a Heinz-variety gelding who made it big in the Olympics as a jumper. That's a one-in-a-million shot.''

"Altair's unique.''

"He's trouble with a capital 'T,' Mr. Reese.'' She pulled up the file, frowning. "Jean didn't make these notes for nothing. He has excellent ability to size up a Grand Prix candidate for the jumping circuit.''

"Then why did he agree to show Altair if he thought the stallion was such a loss?"

It was Dany's turn to give him a withering smile. "Because Jean thought he could ride anything and make it win."

"He has—so far. But," he hesitated, tilting his head, watching her with a more gentle expression. "I've been following his career the last four years, and it seems to me he had one hell of a trainer behind the scenes working the kinks out of these animals before they ever showed." He pointed at her. "You're the real reason why he's skyrocketed to fame and has winner after winner on his hands."

She couldn't stand still a moment longer, unable to bear remembering the last four miserable years of her life. "Please— "

He reached out, capturing her arm and turning her toward him. Dany was wildly aware of his masculine aura and she pulled her arm away. "I made a mistake by hiring three different male trainers to coach Altair. He needs a woman's touch."

She took a step away. "Doesn't every male," she noted with sarcasm. "I have no wish to get mangled by that sorrel stallion. I've heard rumors that Altair has injured all his trainers to some degree.''

"And in every instance it was their fault," he growled. "He's an intelligent horse who won't be beaten or cajoled into doing something. He has to be reasoned with psychologically and respected."

"I have no wish to end up with a broken neck or fractured skull because of that red devil!"

"You're reacting to rumors, that's all."

Danielle's eyes widened, their blueness becoming clouded with cobalt flecks. How could this— this "cowboy" from California suddenly walk in unannounced and demand that she fulfill this agreement made so long ago? The only business that she wanted to conduct today was to turn over control of the Virginia training and stable business to her new partner. Had it only been nine months since the divorce from Jean Baptiste Daguerre? Her heart wrenched in anger and pain over the shock of his sudden departure. Jean was the brilliant, flamboyant part of their duo, and she was only the trainer who stayed behind the scenes doing the groundwork and strenuous training of thoroughbreds for their blue-blooded owners of the East Coast. Jean had ridden nearly every one of the horses she had lovingly trained to the very heights of equine stardom. He would show them in stadium jumping, dressage and the dangerous, spectacular three-day cross-country eventing. The more dangerous, the more closely timed the event, the better his electric performance on the horse. Choking down a lump forming in her throat, she was unable to meet Sam Reese's inquiring gaze. It was too bad Jean's performance in their marriage had gotten such poor marks. She sighed. It was just as much her fault; she spent too much time training the young horses and too little time with Jean.

"My attorneys have made inquiries as to Mr. Daguerre's whereabouts, and they've informed me he has left for a series of commitments in France. I have a Grand Prix hopeful standing in my barn, Mrs. Daguerre, and when your ex-husband saw Altair last year, he said he'd campaign him." He gave a slight shrug of his shoulders. "Fortunately, you haven't left the States and your credentials are well respected in this country. I don't care who fulfills the commitment." His voice, husky and low, hardened. "But one of you will. I haven't spent thousands of dollars on this stallion to see him wasted in the hands of some second-class amateur."

Dany shook her head. "I'm a trainer, Mr. Reese, not a show rider. There's a big difference."

His face was darkly tanned, chiseled as if sculpted by the sun and wind. He looked as though he would be at ease with any element that nature could conjure up. There was a faint look of surprise in his challenging gaze. "You can double as both."

Dany uncrossed her arms, holding them stiffly at her sides. She wasn't going to honor any commitment signed by Jean! "I'm too tall, Mr. Reese! Most of your riders are five-five to five-seven. Even the male riders are usually around a hundred and forty pounds. I'm one forty and my weight will cause the horse to tire on a long and demanding cross-country course. And my height would interfere with the horse's movement, especially if he's sixteen hands or less. You can't mix and match something like this, you know."

He relaxed against the door jamb, oddly out of place in his western attire. "I wouldn't change one inch or pound on you," he murmured appreciatively, making a thorough appraisal of her body.

Dany colored fiercely, getting ready to unleash a blast of anger at the lazily smiling westerner. "How—"

"Now calm down," he defended. "I meant it as a compliment. You eastern women all seem to be a little uptight. Anyway, Altair is seventeen hands high and can easily carry you. Even with your height, you have that grace and flexibility which can only contribute to some of the more intricate jumps that have to be scaled. So you see, there's no problem there."

She stood rooted to the spot, her body drawn into a stiff posture. She didn't realize that it made her look elegantly classical in her black knee-high English riding boots, white long-sleeved blouse and canary yellow riding breeches. The blouse set off the rich, shining blackness of her hair and accented the natural ruddiness of her complexion. Her thin brows knitted in displeasure. "Your horse could be eighteen hands tall, and I still wouldn't ride him!" she hurled back, her voice quivering with anger. "And you can keep your low opinion of easterners to yourself, Mr. Reese. Now, if you'll excuse me, I'm handing over the reins of this place to my new partner, who's due to arrive any minute now." She walked determinedly up to him, angrily holding his amused gaze.

"I don't think he'll mind waiting," he drawled, remaining between her and the door.

She planted her hands on her hips, glaring up at his ruggedly handsome face. If they had met under other circumstances, she would have found him devastatingly intriguing She had still not gotten over her anger at Jean's impulsive departure, and her life had no place for a man. In fact, she found herself agitated at men in general since the divorce. She wanted to slap his rugged face for the open expression of enjoyment that she saw there.

"If you don't move, I'll—"

"You're worse than a female mountain lion that's been woke up too early in the morning and is starving for a fresh kill," he drawled. "And before you cock that fist at me I think I'd better inform you that I'm your new partner, Mrs. Daguerre."

Danielle's lips parted, and she took a step back, staring up at him in shock. "What? But... the contract was signed by Mr. Jack Ferguson. I don't understand. I thought he bought..."

Sam Reese straightened up and slipped his large hand around her upper arm, gently guiding her back to the desk chair and sat her down. "I own the Sierra Corporation," he explained, resting his bulk on the edge of the desk, watching her closely.

Touching her brow in confusion, she gave him a guarded look of distrust. The man sitting before her was both powerful and rich to own a corporation the size of Sierra. Even though the selling price on half interest of the stable had been more than fair, she found that most of the money would immediately be sent to bill collectors on past due notices. That was another item that Jean had forgotten to mention: He hadn't handled the finances very well, and she found out by accident that the magnitude of the mismanagement totaled near a hundred thousand dollars. It had been the last factor to split their foundering marriage. And it meant selling the controlling interest of her dream: Richland Stables. Something she had slaved and toiled for all her twenty-nine years of life. Richland sat nestled between the rolling, gentle hills of Virginia, two hundred acres of luxurious slopes that were ideal for training young jumpers. Sighing, Danielle forced her thoughts back to the present and to this man who seemed to shadow her like a hound straight from hell.

She buried her face in her hands for a moment, trying to collect her broken, fragmented thoughts. He must have taken her gesture as one of utter defeat.

"Look," he murmured. "I apologize for dropping it on you like this. I can see you're tired and you've had quite a rough month. My half brother

Jack Ferguson signed the sales agreement on your stable. He sent photos of your facility to my ranch out in California six months ago because he knew I was looking for a base of operation back East for Altair. I bought it sight unseen.''

She felt the sting of tears prickling at the back of her eyes, and she shut them tightly, fighting back the deluge of emotion that threatened to engulf her. Why couldn't he be flip or arrogant like Jean? That always brought out her anger, and she was able to withstand any barrage. But this man— he was throwing her completely off base. His work-roughened fingers slipped around her wrist, pulling her hand gently away from her face.

"Here," he growled, "you might need this," and placed a white handkerchief in her palm.

A new, more disturbing sensation coursed electrically through her. Danielle looked up, her lashes thickly matted with tears. His face seemed open and undisguised of intrigue or game playing. He was so diametrically opposite of Jean that it was crumbling her defenses more quickly than she could replace them. This perfect stranger was leaning across the desk, his features sympathetic, offering her solace. She blinked twice and then murmured, "Thank you." She dabbed at her eyes, clenching the linen cloth tightly within her long, artistic fingers.

"Look, Danielle—may I call you that? Westerners hate formality." He gave her a frank smile. "We're mostly homesteader folk and would rather sit down over a whiskey and discuss our troubles. I'll take you to lunch, and we can discuss this problem over some good food. Besides, you look a little shook up."

She shivered inwardly as he spoke her name. It rolled off his tongue like a soft growl of that mountain lion he had mentioned. Her heart was aching, and at the moment, she was aware of only pain and loss.

"Come on," he urged, pulling her to her feet. "You're getting paler by the second. Don't worry. Everything will turn out all right."

Danielle sat quietly in the darkened restaurant, a glass of wine in front of her. She stared down at the salad, her appetite nonexistent.

"You know, if you don't eat, you aren't going to be any good for me," Sam murmured, setting the fork down and wiping his mouth with the cloth napkin.

Her eyes widened. "What?"

"I have a proposal for you," he began. "And one that I think might do you a lot of good." He rested his elbows on the table, leaning forward. "Fly back to my ranch that sits above Placerville and work Altair for me throughout the late spring. Then, if he comes along under your hand, I'll put him on any show circuit you want. I can even have you both flown back East here for the Devon show. What do you say?"

She took a drink of the wine, trying to shore up her broken defenses. "Your ranch?" she echoed.

Sam sipped the whiskey, the shadows playing across his face reminding her of a medieval knight who had just stepped out of the past into the present and into her life.

"The Cross Bar-U sits in the High Sierra mountains eight thousand feet above Placerville and close to the Truckee River. It's God's unaltered handiwork up there. The Truckee is one of the most violent rivers in the West, and the mountains are some of the finest in the world. I have thousands of acres of rich grassland, steep hills and rolling meadows perfect for training Altair. It's a vast, virgin country, Danielle. Far different than your tame hills here in Virginia." He allowed himself a small smile, his voice vibrating with a low-key excitement. "You would have a suite of rooms at the main house."

She found herself being pulled along by the fervor in his voice. She colored as he picked up one of her hands, pressing it between his own.

"Danielle, you're one of the best trainers in the U.S. when it comes to polishing off an event horse."

Her pulse accelerated unevenly, and she was acutely aware of the strong, callused fingers capturing her hand. His voice was a husky balm to her shredded heart, and his touch soothed her frantic, worried mind. Hesitantly, she withdrew her hand, tucking it in her lap, unable to meet his warm, inviting eyes that seemed to be dappled with silver flecks of excitement.

"My ex-husband was the rider, Mr.—"

"Call me Sam. And frankly, Danielle, I've had a thorough check made into both your backgrounds. Your ex-husband took chances with the horses under his tutelage. The sprained ligaments, the bowed tendons...no, you were the one who brought those animals along and gave them their distance to go that extra mile when it was asked of them. Look, I wouldn't trust anyone else with Altair. He's an athletic, daring stallion who can go all the way. But he's a sensitively calibrated instrument also. He needs your touch. He can't be mishandled at this stage by a whip or a club in some man's hands. You're the only one who can do it."

She touched her hair in confusion, pushing a strand behind her ear that had escaped from the severe chignon she wore while training and riding. Her hair was nearly long enough to reach her slender waist and had to be tightly knotted at the nape of her neck so that she could get her protective hard hat on her head. "Sam—" Her voice quavered and she gave a slight shrug of her shoulders. "Please—so much is happening—I can't think straight. Give me time...."

"I can't do that. Not under the circumstances. Look, you'll love the Sierras. I believe the change of location and environment might do you a world of good. Might bring back that sparkle to your blue eyes and put a dash of color on those pale cheeks." He stared at her intently for a moment. "It may make you smile again. You have a beautiful mouth."

Danielle shivered at the husky inference in his tone. There was a veiled, hungry look in his gray eyes, and she stared wordlessly across the table at him, feeling her body respond of its own volition to the invitation. "I just can't pack up and leave Richland! I have several coming five-year-olds here that need daily training and—"

"You have two capable assistants," he countered. "Surely they can manage the three animals that are here."

She sighed heavily. Since Jean had left, the bulk of their numerous clientele had left Richland. She wished that their clients had known that it was her ability that had made those horses winners. But she couldn't ride—at least that's what Jean had always impressed upon her—and clients didn't want just a good trainer, they wanted a brilliant rider to make their horse a winner. And she was anything but a brilliant show rider.

"I'd be willing to invest fifty thousand in Richland for renovation purposes plus an advertising campaign that will bring you in some of the biggest clients in the world. You give me four months of your time and I'll make sure Richland becomes a center for Grand Prix hopefuls on both sides of the Atlantic."

She stared in shock at him. Fifty thousand...what she could do with that money! It would enable her to buy another hot-walker to cool out her charges after their demanding morning runs, another groom to help in the more mundane duties around the barn and—it was too good to turn down.

"Look," she began unevenly, "the offer is wonderful, and to tell you the truth, it would help Richland." She lifted her lashes, meeting his steady gaze, her heart beating painfully in her breast. "Sam, I'm *not* a show rider. Oh, sure, I can ride. But I'm not a Grand Prix rider. I have no experience . . . no—"

"Who told you that?" he demanded quietly. "You train world-class hunters and jumpers and you stand here and tell me with such incredible humbleness that you can't ride them?" Disbelief flared in his gray eyes.

Dany chewed on her lower lip, evading his extraordinary eyes. She could lose herself in their pewter color. "I'd rather not discuss it."

He sat back, a quizzical expression written on his features. The seconds strung tautly between them. He watched her silently for a moment. "You ever seen Altair?"

She shook her head. "No."

"Hell, I'll change the deal. You fly back with me and take a look at him. If he doesn't sell you on staying at the Cross Bar-U and riding him in shows, then I'll let you come back East. Deal?" He held out his large hand toward her.

Danielle's lips parted, and she stared down at his hand. She could come back to Virginia if she didn't like the horse. "You'd release me from the contract if I'm not impressed with Altair?" she hedged carefully. "And still put the fifty thousand into the stable?"

Sam nodded his head. "That's right, Danielle. Now, we got a deal?"

She slipped her hand into the warmth of his. "Deal," she murmured.

Sam reluctantly released his hold and leaned back, smiling boyishly. "Welcome to the Sierras, Danielle. You're going to love it there."

Two

"Martha," Sam thundered as he walked into the main foyer of the ranch house, "we're home."

Dany stole a look around at his so-called ranch house. It was a magnificent two-story castle, reminding her of the grand haciendas of the Spanish dons in California during the eighteenth century. The red tile floor gleamed dully beneath their feet, and the halls were made of dark rough wood, accentuating the definite masculinity of the interior. She followed Sam down the hall, and he led her into a sitting room. Everywhere she looked she noticed oil paintings of family members. It was obvious from the rich furnishings and age of the ranch that it had all been handed down for at least a century, coming finally to the man who now stood before her.

"She must be in the kitchen, Danielle. Sit down and rest. I'll be right back."

"I think I'll stand, Sam. I need some exercise to shake off the tiredness."

He nodded, putting down two of her suitcases. "We'll remedy that very shortly. I hope you're ready to see the best eventing hunter in the U.S."

She had to smile at his unabashed enthusiasm. "Whenever you are," she assured him. She wanted to add that it didn't matter, having made up her mind to decline training Altair. Tomorrow morning she would leave for Virginia. As lovely and rugged as the drive to the ranch was, it contrasted startlingly with the gentleness inherent in Virginia woodland. Even though tall redwoods and spruce towered over the small, winding highway leading up to the Cross Bar-U and the fragrance of pine refreshed her senses, the snow-capped mountains looked like giant predators surrounding her. Where could she possibly ride a horse in those jagged peaks?

Martha came flying around the corner, her skirt rustling, a wooden spoon in one hand and a ball of bread dough in the other. She was a short plump woman, reminiscent of a pigeon. She stared across the room at Dany. "Oh, lordy!" she exclaimed, her applelike cheeks glowing pink from the heat of the kitchen. "Where's Sam! Oh, you must be Mrs. Daguerre. I didn't expect you for another hour!" She frowned, turning on her heel. "Sam! Where are you? I swear, you're worse than a little boy. Spring'n surprises on me like this. Wait till I—"

Dany put her hand over her mouth to suppress a smile as Sam wandered back into the room. Martha couldn't be more than five feet tall, and Sam towered over her like a redwood in comparison. The housekeeper waved her wooden spoon threateningly up at him. "Sam Reese, if you were twenty-five years younger, I'd take you across my knee, boy! The very idea of coming an hour early!" she scolded.

Sam took off his hat, grinning contentedly, a twinkle in his eyes as he glanced over at Dany. "This is Martha. She's been with our family all of her life. She more or less runs the household, and me," he added drolly. "I think the last time I got hit with her wooden spoon was when I was ten years old."

Martha belligerently placed her hand on her hip. "And it isn't like you didn't have it coming, Sam Reese."

Dany laughed heartily, wiping the tears from her eyes, watching the two of them stand there self-consciously. "I had no idea Sam was such a rambunctious youngster."

Martha glared back up at her full-grown charge. "He still is. He still is. Listen, Sam, you take Mrs.—"

"Please, call me Dany," she offered.

Sam raised one eyebrow speculatively. "Dany? Nice nickname," he complimented her huskily.

"Most of my friends know me as Dany," she explained. "Or, you can call me Danielle, Martha. Whichever is easiest. I'll answer to just about anything."

Martha dipped her head. "Just don't answer late for dinner, Dany. I only ring that bell once!"

"Believe me," she assured the feisty housekeeper, barely able to contain a smile, "I won't. I don't want to get whacked with a spoon."

Martha blushed furiously. "Oh, I'd never do that!" She waved it up in Sam's general direction. "He knows I'm just like an old hunting dog with no teeth left. All bark and no bite."

"Most of the time," Sam kidded. He held out his hand toward Dany. "Martha will make sure the boys bring in your gear. Come on, I'll show you where you'll be staying."

When Sam Reese said a suite of rooms, he meant exactly that. The ranch house was large, but because of the homey atmosphere and earthiness of colors throughout it, it seemed smaller and more intimate to her. Sam opened a door on the second floor, urging her in. She stood inside the room, her eyes widening in appreciation. He halted at her shoulder, watching her expression with a look of pleasure in his eyes.

"Well, do you think this will do? Over here you have a full bath including a whirlpool." He looked down at her. "That's for times when you bite the dust and you're sore."

She laughed. "Are you trying to tell me that Altair is accustomed to throwing his riders?"

"He's a handful," he remarked cryptically. "And the next room, which incidentally joins my suite, is a living room." He opened another door. There was a set of large windows with the beige drapes pulled back to allow a cascade of sunshine to spill into the pale green room. Dany stood there, admiring it silently.

"It's lovely, Sam." She tilted her head, catching his pleased expression. "And flowers!" A delicate blue vase in the center of the pecan table seemed to overflow with blossoms. She walked over to the table, caressing one of the petals.

"Those come from the property here. With the snow leaving and the temperature starting to rise, they're popping up all over the place. Martha picked them especially for you. She said ladies from the East would appreciate flowers."

Leaning over them, she cupped them within her hands and inhaled their fragrance. She closed her eyes, murmuring, "I never expected such a warm welcome."

"Part of the Western tradition," he assured her. "You're like one of the family now, you know. Martha will treat you like a daughter and dote on you, if you let her." He hesitated at the other door leading to his suite. "Listen, you rest for a while, and later, when you come down, I'll take you out to see Altair."

Dany straightened up, her eyes giving away the excitement she felt. "I would like to rest. But I'm dying to see Altair...."

"He can wait two more hours. Now get changed into something more comfortable and take a nap."

"Is that an order?"

"No, just a strong suggestion."

Dany tossed her head, laughing. "It's good advice. I'll see you later, Sam."

He dipped his head and opened the door. "Look, if you need anything, just come on in. I'm going to be slaving over some paperwork that's built up over the last week."

Dany unpacked one suitcase, leaving the others sitting where the ranch hands had placed them. She hung up her black silk robe and tucked her toiletry articles in the bathroom. Changing into a pair of russet-colored jodhpurs and a yellow blouse, she loosened her ebony hair, allowing it to flow freely across her shoulders. The queen-size bed looked inviting, and against her better judgment, she lay down on it, intent on resting about twenty minutes before viewing the stallion.

New sounds, sounds of cattle lowing plaintively and of horses whickering in friendly fashion, lulled her into a restful state. She had not meant to sleep, but the sun was warm against her back as she curled up on the huge expanse of the bed, and weeks of emotional exhaustion were placed into limbo.

Danielle moaned, hearing herself cry out. "No!" she screamed. The voice, her voice, reverberated into her restless, sleeping state, and she choked off another cry. In the dream, she saw herself transformed into a horse who was being whipped cruelly by the handler. The horse struggled, trying to escape the biting flick of the whip that Jean had in his hand. Pain seared her heart and she moaned. Jean was yelling, driving her back into a corner. She was trying to escape the whip and the pain.

"Dany?" a new voice called. The husky, warm voice sliced again into the anguish of the nightmare. She whimpered, feeling the caress of a man's hand against her arm, moving up across her shoulder in a caring fashion. "Dany, wake up. You're having a bad dream."

She gasped, blinking open her eyes. Sam Reese sat on the edge of the bed leaning across, his hand resting on her shoulder. Tearstains glistened against her cheeks, and he reached over, touching her skin with his fingers, making an awkward attempt to remove the wetness.

"You're all right, lady," he soothed. "You were crying out and I heard you next door. Just take it easy. Everything is going to be fine."

The rough caress of his fingers against her face sent a new, aching sensation through her tense body. The musky scent of his masculine body invaded her nostrils, and her heart pounded without restraint. She was captured by the tenderness of his expression, his eyes broadcasting genuine concern. Dany shivered, confused by his care and affection. She pushed his hand away, struggling to sit up and get away from his powerful male body.

"I'm all right," she gulped, rubbing her face. Her hair fell in blue black sheets about her pale features.

Sam nodded, watching her in silence for long moments. He caressed the crown of her head, his hand barely skimming the surface of her hair. "I was right," he murmured softly, "you have lovely hair, Dany. You ought to wear it down more often. Makes you look like a princess." A bashful smile pulled one corner of his mouth, and he hesitantly drew his hand away, resting it against his thigh.

It took a few moments to retrieve her senses. The sun was no longer shining and darkness had claimed the day. She was excruciatingly aware of Sam Reese as he sat quietly beside her, making no further attempt to touch her. Finally, she raised her head, meeting his gaze.

"I'm sorry," she apologized in a thick voice.

"What for? We all have bad dreams every once in a while. I've put you through a great deal in just a few days time, Dany, and it's caught up with you."

She shook her head. "No, it wasn't you," she whispered. "Oh, I'll admit it's been hectic and surprising, but that wasn't it." She gave a broken, helpless shrug. "Just the past coming back to haunt me again. As usual."

He pursed his lips, nodding sagely. "You know there's one sure cure for the past."

"What's that?"

"Get involved in the present. Let the past go. It's dead and gone. You did what you had to do and gave it your best shot." He forced a weak smile. "Take my word for it, I've been there, too."

Dany chewed on her lower lip, glancing at him. His face was so strong, and yet, an innate gentleness burned in the depth of his slate gray eyes. There was inbred harshness in the lines of his thirty-five-year-old face. The lines which gave his face character had obviously been earned. The furrowed, broad forehead had seen worry, and the creases that fanned from the corner of each eye and the lines around his mouth spoke of laughter, laughter that she wished she could share with him. She gasped at the sudden, unexpected thought, and he must have mistaken her reaction.

"Getting divorced isn't the end of the world," he said. "I had my turn at it, too. Tried to put a thoroughbred in a plow horse's harness, and it just didn't work."

Dany smiled tentatively at the expression, watching his eyes cloud with unspoken memories. "I like the way you westerners talk, Sam. You seem to put everything into such simple perspective."

It was his turn to share a smile, and he clasped her hand, giving it a squeeze. "Simple but effective," he agreed, sliding off the bed and standing. "Why don't you take a bath and gradually get yourself back together? Dinner won't be for another hour."

"But what about Altair?"

Sam looked out the window and walked over to the drapes, drawing them closed. "Tomorrow morning is the earliest you're doing anything. If you'd like, I'll have Martha send up a tray and you can eat here."

"That sounds wonderful, Sam. I hope I didn't ruin any plans you had for dinner...."

"No. I always eat alone anyway. Besides, your comfort comes first."

"I appreciate your thoughtfulness. What time can we go see Altair tomorrow?"

"Whenever you get up. He's in the stud barn that sits across from the bunkhouse. Chances are, you'll sleep in tomorrow."

"I've got news for you. Trainers are up around four-thirty with the dawn. If I sleep past six, I'll be surprised."

He nodded. "Well, I'll leave you be for now. Good night, Dany."

She heard the tenor in his voice, and it made her want to ask him to stay. The loneliness was evident in the look he gave her, and yet, he wasn't going to force his will upon her. How vastly different from Jean!

After a delicious meal of beef rump roast, potatoes and peas that Martha brought up, Dany took a long, fragrant bath and then slipped back into bed for the night. This time there were no bad dreams. Only an aching remembrance of Sam's hand on her cheek wiping her tears away.

Three

She awoke exactly at four-thirty. Dawn was barely breaking its hold on the night as Dany tiptoed downstairs to the kitchen. To her surprise, the coffee had already been made. She poured herself a cup, putting cream and sugar in it, and then walked quietly out the back door. A thin blanket of fog hovered a few feet off the ground throughout the valley. The ranch sat on the southern end of the valley, surrounded on all sides by a thick forest of pines. The restless snort of horses waiting for their feeding hour was a welcome sound. Pulling her coat around her more tightly, Dany grasped the handle of the mug and meandered in the direction of the paddocks and the stable.

Her hair swung with the natural rhythm of her body, the shorter tendrils framing her face from the dampness of the early morning humidity created by the ground fog. She turned the corner of the bunkhouse, catching sight of Sam leaning up against the fence. Dany stopped, her breath catching in her breast as she drank in his unmoving form. The brim of the hat was drawn down across his eyes, the denim jacket molded against the broad expanse of his shoulders and back. One leg was cocked lazily on the last rung of the fence, and he held a steaming mug of coffee in both hands as he seemed to be watching something in the distance. Her gaze traveled the meadow that disappeared out into the white blanket.

There, not much more than a mile away, she could barely make out an outline of a horse standing alertly. She watched as Sam put his fingers to his mouth. A shrill whistle broke the morning stillness. She heard the answering call; the unmistakable bugling scream of a stallion. Sam set the coffee mug on the post and climbed into the paddock, walking toward the horse who appeared magically out of the fog.

Dany shivered as she watched the man and the stallion come together. Sam walked unconcernedly as the giant red stallion strained forward like a huge unstoppable freight train that had no brakes. She stifled a cry of warning, watching the sorrel suddenly veer off to the right and playfully scramble in a circle about the man. It had to be Altair! She released her held breath, awed by the sight of the magnificent thoroughbred. Altair reared, pawing his front legs through the air, and then came down only a few feet from Sam, snorting vehemently. It was as if the two males were squaring off at one another, each king of his own special domain. Danielle stood transfixed by the beauty and rugged handsomeness of the spectacle. Sam spoke in a quiet, firm tone to the stallion, holding out his hand. Altair's small ears twitched, and he turned his intelligent eyes upon the man, snorting again. Pawing restlessly, the stallion flicked his thick flaxen tail, and bent his head to take the treat.

She walked toward them as Altair nibbled the offering from Sam's hand. By the time she got to the fence, they had both seen her. Sam put his arm across the stallion's neck and led him over to the fence.

"Good morning. I see you caught us at our favorite game."

"For a moment I thought he was going to run you over," she admitted.

"He's been known to do that to people he didn't like. Come here, Altair. I want to introduce your new rider and trainer." He pulled the horse by the mane, and the stallion docilely complied.

Dany flinched inwardly at the word "rider." She did not share Sam's belief that she could be one. Her eyes widened in appreciation, noting the thoroughbred's impeccable conformation. Altair nuzzled her arm, his nostrils flaring as he caught her scent. She watched him carefully; she never really trusted any stallion. They were male animals ruled by an instinctive sexual drive and not capable of thinking, only reacting.

Sam stood back, admiring both of them, his hands on his hips. "He certainly seems to take to you. Of course, he'd be stupid not to."

Dany smiled distantly, keenly assessing the stallion's personality, watching his ears and the look in his large brown eyes. "He's far from stupid, Sam. And I can see he allows very few people to tell him what to do."

Sam laughed, joining her at the fence. "No one *tells* Altair a thing. They have to *ask*." And then he frowned, picking up his coffee mug and taking a sip from it. "Which is where I've run into a lot of trouble with his riders lately. They treat him like an unthinking animal with only four legs and the power of a runaway truck. They don't realize he's thinking in his own terms and his forte is correctly judging complicated jumps. He's a dynamic hunter who will challenge everything except a water obstacle."

Dany ran her fingers down the stallion's sleek, silky neck, enjoying the play of muscles beneath his skin. She noted with a sinking feeling that long thin scars marred his beautiful copper coat. "My God, who did this to him?" she whispered, running her fingers along one scar that ran the length of his left shoulder. Her heart turned over in compassion as she noted several more scars around his mouth and across the top of his nose.

Sam came around, affectionately scratching Altair's ears. "Remember me telling you that the wrangler who captured him tried to break his spirit?" he asked huskily.

Dany looked up, aware of the simmering anger hidden in his voice and reflected in his eyes. "This is outright cruelty!" she protested, her voice strangled with emotion. Gently, she reached up, caressing Altair's scarred muzzle. The stallion moved away from her hand, the white of his eye showing as he took another step backward. She shook her head. "I don't blame him for jerking away," she said tightly. "What did they do, use wire to try and keep his head and nose down?"

"Yes. It didn't work, but it made him head shy with everyone except me." Sam gave her a smile of encouragement. "And I think he'll eventually let you touch his mouth without going crazy. I can see he's already responding to you in a way he's never done before with anyone else."

"Typical male."

"Yes, and thank God you're the one to help him over some of his worst faults," Sam said fervently. "Altair may not appreciate your beauty, but I do." He grinned and playfully put his arm across the stallion's neck and leaned against him.

"How do you get the bit into his mouth if he's head shy?"

Sam pursed his mouth, casting a troubled glance in her direction. "Very carefully. We use the snaffle only when he shows in the dressage portion of the show."

Dany gave him an incredulous look. "What on earth do you use, then?" It was beyond comprehension in her mind to ride an eventing horse without a bit in his mouth! Riding over a thou-

sand pounds of horseflesh at twenty-five to thirty
miles an hour over a grueling, dangerous course
without the control of a bit was impossible to
comprehend. No wonder Altair has injured his
previous riders, she thought, experiencing a sinking feeling in the pit of her stomach.

"We use an aluminum hackamore, Dany."

She searched her memory for the use of the
training device. Hackamores were invented for the
horse that wouldn't carry a bit in its mouth. The
rawhide or aluminum loop fit around the muzzle
and when it was pulled on, it exerted pressure
against sensitive nerve endings that lay on either
cheek of the horse's jaw. She gave Sam a distrustful look. "Is that why the riders have been injured?"

"No. Do you think I'd ask you to ride and train
him if he wasn't manageable?" he demanded.

She bristled. "At this moment, I think anything is possible! You bind me with a contract that
was signed by my ex-husband and practically
blackmail me to fly me out here to retrain this
horse." She was aware of the effort he was making to control his temper as his gray eyes darkened like ominous thunderclouds.

"I'm not in the habit of risking people's lives,
particularly a woman who I think can salvage my

stallion and bring him into his own. I need you
alive, not dead, Dany. Sure, he can be dangerous
because of his past. But he's responsive. Altair is
not deliberately cruel or vicious. God knows, he
ought to be, for what he's suffered. But look at
him. Does he look unsafe?"

As if listening to the heated conversation between them, Altair walked between them, head
down, standing quietly while they glared across his
back at one another. Dany put her hands on her
hips in defiance.

"I won't ride him unless he's got a bit in his
mouth, that's final."

"Fine. You find a way to do it, and we'll both
be happy. He's extremely responsive to the hackamore, though."

She shook her head. "Sam Reese, either you're
the most eccentric man I've ever met with an even
more eccentric horse or—"

"We're both unique," he interrupted. His gaze
lingered on her. "And so are you. You're one of a
kind, lady. Just the gal to help Altair to become
the best Grand Prix jumper in the world."

She didn't know how to react to his back-
handed compliments, and was continually un-
comfortable beneath his warming, caressing gaze.

"Tell me what else he has problems with," she muttered. "The fly in the ointment, no doubt."

"He doesn't like water. He'll damn near do anything to avoid it. Including dumping his rider into an oxer or earth bank."

Dany looked over at him. "Did your riders quit, or were they killed?"

Sam managed a sour grin. "None killed. One got hurt pretty seriously, and he was out of action for two months. It was after Tony's fall that I decided I wasn't going to risk anyone's life until I could get Richland Stables to honor its commitment."

Dany frowned, allowing Altair to nuzzle her hair with his velvety nose. "Are you going to let me help you, big boy?" she asked the stallion, giving him a playful pat on the forehead. Altair backed away, snorting. A mare from another pasture whickered a greeting, and the sorrel thoroughbred raised his magnificent head, standing like a marble statue. He bugled out an answering call, the sound raucous and harsh to their ears. Sam smiled and slipped between the railings.

"That's his way of making sweet talk to them."

"He's a nice-looking horse, Sam. So I can't blame the mares for wanting to entice him over to their paddocks," she grudgingly admitted.

He took her arm and led her down toward the stable. "We've got his yearling crop in here. I bred him to five of my best broodmares. Let's see what you think of the results." Dany reviewed the thoroughbred yearlings and stood in the passage between the large, roomy boxstalls with Sam. "That's simply amazing," she admitted. "There's a uniformity in conformation I've rarely seen. Each one looks like a stamp of Altair."

"Exactly. He's prepotent as hell. I bred him to five different bloodlines to see how his genes would affect the mare's breeding line. In every case, his stamp came out," Sam said, sounding somewhat incredulous. "The legs on every yearling are absolutely straight. They're bred to withstand the strain of jumping."

Dany smiled. "And you can hardly wait for them to mature enough to put them on the circuit, right?"

He walked her out of the barn, and they ambled at a slow pace toward the house. The sun was barely edging the tip of the Sierras, sending streamers of light through the fog as the thickened mist began to evaporate. The cobalt blue sky turned a shade paler as the sun ascended across the peaks, promising another cool spring day. She was aware of his body only inches from her own, and once again, her skin prickled with a pleasurable tingle as his arm occasionally brushed against her.

Halting at the back porch, he pushed the hat off his forehead, watching her closely. "Well, what do you think? Is he reason enough to stay on?"

She avoided his gray eyes. Instead, she turned her back to him, drawing in a deep, steadying breath. "Please don't think my decision has anything to do with Altair's conformation or potential, Sam." She girded herself inwardly, closing her eyes tightly for a moment. "But I can't stay. This is too strange an environment for me to stay here. I'm used to the Eastern circuit, and I'm familiar with the people and the land."

"You're the only woman capable of bringing Altair around," he growled.

Dany gritted her teeth. The man was stubborn! Irritation stirred to life within her, and she compressed her lips and turned, meeting his fiery gaze. Part of her resolve disappeared immediately. Sam Reese was no longer pleasant-looking in any sense of the word. He was towering over her, his eyes an angry silver hue. She took a step back, feeling the masculine aura of strength so sharply that it made her dizzy.

"It's not the training aspect that bothers me," she managed, her voice strident.

"Then what the hell is it?"

She opened her mouth and then closed it, her sapphire eyes glittering with golden fire. Why did she want to escape? Was she running from Sam? Or her fear of having to ride in shows? She sensed her body's own hungry needs that had lain dormant for over nine months. She didn't want a careless affair with him. He was able to manipulate her as no other man ever had, and it frightened her thoroughly. "I'm turning your offer down, it's as simple as that."

Sam smiled savagely. "Nothing's as simple as that, Mrs. Daguerre. Remember, there's been a contract signed, and I'll hold you to it if I have to."

Her nostrils flared with contempt. "You wouldn't dare!"

"What are you running from?" he asked, his voice suddenly lined with impatience. He reached out, grabbing her arm and drawing her near. "Sorry," he breathed thickly, "but you're too good a trainer and I need you for that horse out there. I don't care what you're running from, but you aren't leaving this commitment. You'll fulfill the obligations.''

Dany muffled a curse, jerking her arm away from his branding fingers of fire on her skin. "You—you bastard," she hissed. "All right," she blurted out in reckless abandon, "I'll stay! But keep away from me while I'm training that horse. Do you hear me? I don't want a thing to do with you!''

She rubbed her bruised arm, taking two more steps away from him. God, how she hated that composed, implacable look on his stony face. How had she led herself to think it was as simple as flying out to his ranch? His tenderness and care from the night before had thrown her off guard. Well, his true personality was now surfacing. He was just as arrogant and imperious as that stallion of his. Her lips curled away from her teeth. "I despise you for thinking you can run my life for me, Mr. Reese. You're so used to molding everything to the way you want it. It's obvious you come from generations of men who are used to getting their way. Well, you may get your way for a while, but as soon as I'm done with Altair, I'm leaving. And I don't care if I have to run away in the dead of night to do it!''

Sam smiled lazily, beginning to relax. He pulled the brim of the cowboy hat down across his eyes. "If you leave, you'll find yourself in high country full of cougar, bear and bobcat. And at this time of year, they're coming out of a hard winter and they're hungry. So forget that idea."

Four

The next morning Dany woke up, determined to get to work on Altair. She threw on her hunt breeches, knee-high black riding boots, and grabbed her protective hard hat and leather gloves. Stopping in the kitchen, she borrowed a jar of molasses from Martha and headed determinedly out to the stud barn.

Cowboys dressed in blue chambray shirts, dusty, dirty jeans or well-worn chaps looked with mild interest as she walked briskly into dark passages between the boxstalls. Dany halted for a moment, allowing her eyes to adjust to the dim-

ness. She found Altair in his stall and placed the
jump saddle and other riding equipment down
beside the ties. She still felt testy and belligerent
from her confrontation with Sam yesterday, and
she sent a warning glance at one cowboy who
started to say something and then, apparently,
thought better of it.

Altair whickered gently as she approached.
"Just like him, aren't you?" she whispered. "All
sweet talk on the outside and mean on the inside.
Come on, it's time for us to get acquainted."

The big red stallion stood quietly in the ties in
the middle of the aisle as she brushed him down
vigorously until his copper coat shone like a newly
minted penny. Two ranch hands sitting down at
the end of the stable watched her in silence, each
chewing on a wad of tobacco lodged in his
weather-hardened cheek. Dany was positive that
they had never seen someone in English riding
clothes, and that irritated her even more. Damn
Sam Reese! The breeze was slight, stirring through
the barn, as she rummaged around until she located the tack room. In there, she found Altair's
hackamore hanging and a snaffle bit beside it.
Fashioning a double bridle composed of the snaffle along with the hackamore, Dany brought out
the bridle and opened the jar of thick, sweet mo-

lasses, spreading the brown syrup onto the snaffle.

"You're going to like this," she muttered. Approaching the curious stallion, Dany placed her right arm between his ears, holding the headstall. With her left hand, she held the snaffle close to the stallion's mouth. His large nostrils flared as he picked up the sweet scent.

"That's right," she crooned, putting the snaffle in the palm of her hand and resting it on his lips. "Easy...easy..." she whispered as he opened his mouth and began licking the molasses off the bit.

Dany gave a sigh of relief as she deftly slid the snaffle into the stallion's mouth, placing the hackamore over his nose and then sliding the headstall behind his small ears. Altair stood there, chomping in an exaggerated fashion as he mouthed the snaffle. Dany remained near, crooning softly to him and patting him. She followed the same procedures ten more times until Altair docilely accepted the bit. The next stage of the plan would be more dangerous; she would not only have to get used to the horse but also balance control through the hackamore and snaffle. Would he rear or flip over backward on her if she pulled too hard on the reins that were attached to the snaffle? Chances of injury on a horse "sun-fishing" on her were great. It would mean leaping off his back at exactly the right moment or getting crushed under a thousand pounds of flailing horse. She slipped the snaffle bit into Altair's mouth one more time and the bridle over his large, broad head and snapped the throatlatch closed. She decided to use a strap attached from the cinch to the noseband known as a standing martingale. It would stop Altair from jerking his head up and hitting her.

Taking a riding crop, Dany slipped it over her wrist and drew on the thin riding gloves. She recalled times when the palms of her hands had been cut open by horses who had pulled the leather reins sharply through her grip. Wearing the gloves protected her hands, plus it gave her more grip with the sometimes slippery reins. Fixing the hard hat firmly on her head, she buckled it tightly, the chin strap snug against her jaw. Looking up at Altair, she muttered, "Okay, big boy, let's find out what you're made of. If it's anything like that owner of yours, this ought to be one heck of an experience for both of us."

Altair brushed her shoulder affectionately, beginning to prance airily as she led him out into the bright afternoon sunshine. He tossed his head, sensing the excitement of his rider. Dany looked around and decided to ride him in a pasture that seemed free of fences at the other end. If she did get in trouble with him, then there was open area to deal with the situation. She placed the toe of her boot in the stirrup, leaping easily upon the stallion's broad back. Altair sidled, tucking his head and humping his rear playfully. Dany monitored the pressure on the hackamore, forcing him to stop the small, harmless bucks. All cross-country horses were bred hot, and few could stand still for more than one second if they were asked. Altair was no different.

The stallion felt good between her tightly clenched thighs, and she carefully moved her calves against his well-sprung barrel, gently putting pressure against him, asking him to move out at a slow trot. A small smile of appreciation smoothed the frown on her features as he moved out in a fluid, unbroken stride. His nostrils flared, drinking in great draughts of wind, as she moved him in large, lazy circles, checking his sense of balance, of motion and flexibility, against the hackamore. He responded beautifully.

For twenty minutes, Dany tested Altair's weaknesses and strengths, finding him an utter delight to ride. Although tall for a rider, she looked like a miniature jockey astride the giant copper stallion, his flaxen mane and tail flowing like white silk behind him. Dany spotted several oxer jumps a good two miles away. Sitting deeply in the seat of the saddle, she pushed downward with her spine, giving him the signal to gallop. Altair surged forward in an unbroken, pounding rhythm. His length of reach was phenomenal, because his legs were long in proportion to his extreme height. The ground began to blur into a ribbon of green, and the wind created by the thoroughbred's speed sheared against Dany's face, causing her eyes to water.

Dany began to pull Altair in, applying just a slight pressure against the snaffle and more against the hackamore as the oxers came up quickly. She reached down, touching his sleek neck and shoulder, checking for sweat; there was none. She was pleased that he was in such good condition and began to croon to the stallion, asking him to slow his pace even more. Raising up off the saddle, knees pushed inward against the small patch of leather, Dany leaned forward on his withers to check his speed even more, her face inches from his arched neck. A small puddle of water appeared over the next small rise, and Altair was suddenly airborne, popping over the puddle as if

it were a jump. Dany's neck snapped back and she
felt her body being pulled back by the mighty
thrust of power from the unexpected leap. Her
thighs tightened like a steel trap against the saddle. Altair landed heavily, startled by the sudden
shift of his rider's weight. She slammed forward,
her face smacking into the crest of the stallion's
neck. For a moment, blackness threatened to engulf her, but she hung on, gripping his mane.

"Whoa," she croaked, sitting up and pulling
him to a stop. Her nose ached abominably, and
she shook her head, trying to escape the pain that
radiated outward from it. She reached up with her
gloved hand. "Oh, damn," she muttered, staring
at the blood on her fingers.

"Problems?" a cool voice inquired.

Dany jerked around in the saddle, startled.

Sam's eyes narrowed and he lost that infuriat-
ing smile when he saw the blood. He kicked the
gelding forward, coming abreast of her and grabbing Altair's reins. She blushed angrily, pinching
her nose shut to try and halt the bleeding, and
jerked the reins out of his hand. "I told you to
leave me alone!" she said.

"You're hurt," he said, his voice losing its
coolness and reflecting genuine care.

"Well it won't be the first or last time."

Sam swore softly, glaring at her. "You're a hellion just like that horse when you want to be. Why don't you climb down off there and let me see how badly hurt—"

Keeping her hand over her nose, Dany kneed Altair, and the stallion made a quick turn. "No thanks! Just stay out of my way. Do you understand me?"

He sat there on his black gelding, his gray eyes sparks of fury. "You two deserve each other," was all he growled, and yanked his horse around, galloping back toward the group of cows and men waiting for him about a mile away.

Tears ran down her cheeks, and she spit out the distasteful metallic taste of blood from her mouth. That would serve her right: She should have checked over the terrain first. It was clear that she would have to begin work in earnest with Altair on all sorts of water situations. She gave him a pat. "Come on, big boy, get me home so I can get a cold cloth on this nose. I hope it's not broken. God, it hurts."

She had managed to remove the bit from Altair's mouth and was trying to unsaddle him when Sam appeared out of nowhere. He lifted the saddle off in one smooth motion and gripped her arm firmly with the other. Dany muffled her protest as he dragged her down the aisle toward the house.

"You might as well quit struggling," he declared grimly, handing the saddle to one of his hands. He stopped long enough to say, "Jake, cool Altair down and then put him back in his paddock."

Dany tried to pull away. Blood was still trickling from her nose, and she put her other hand up to try and halt it. "Let me go!" she cried.

"Stop it," he ordered, pulling her along.

They passed Martha, whose eyes widened with surprise as he guided her through the kitchen. Sam took her to his suite, forcing her to sit down on a stool in the huge bathroom. He threw his hat down and took a washrag, running it under a faucet. Dany sat there, tears streaming down her face, infuriated and embarrassed.

Martha came on the run, panting as she waddled around the bedroom door to the bathroom. "Sam, what's happened to her?"

His fingers slid along Dany's jaw, and she tried to jerk away. "If you don't sit still," he threatened softly, the moistness of his breath fanning across her face, "I'm going to take you over my knee."

Martha crowded in, her keen brown eyes assessing Dany's nose. "I'll go call Dr. Hart right away."

"Do that."

"No!" Dany protested, acutely aware of his strong fingers against her chin and jaw.

"Yes!" Sam thundered to the departing Martha. He glared back down at her. "You're certainly hardheaded." She winced as he gently placed the cloth against her nose. "You may have broken it," he growled, carefully blotting away the blood.

"Oh, shut up!" she mumbled, grabbing the cloth out of his hands. She stood up, examining her nose in the mirror. It was swelling on one side, and she touched it tentatively.

"Why don't you sit down before you fall down and get a damn concussion," he ordered tightly, his eyes broadcasting his concern.

She wasn't going to do one blasted thing he ordered. She might have to live here for a month or two, but that was all! Stubbornly, she remained on her feet, the pain increasing and making her eyes narrow. The cold cloth against her hot skin felt good, and she rinsed out the cloth and put it back against her nose. "You might as well be talking to a wall," she muttered, glaring up at him. "I'm not doing a thing you tell me!"

He leaned forward, his face a mask of tightly controlled fury. "I don't need my rider fainting on me and striking her head against the tile floor of this bathroom. Now sit down before you fall down!"

She wanted to stick her tongue out at him in sheer frustration. He was treating her like a twelve-year-old child. "Don't be ridiculous," she said haughtily. "I'm not going to faint! I've been hurt a lot worse than this and had to take care of myself without anybody's help. So just let me be!"

"That's part of your trouble. You're so self-sufficient that you don't know how to handle someone's offer to help. You've got to be part Irish with stubbornness like that."

His verbal tirade sounded hollow, the words seeming to blur together, and Dany blinked, dropping the cloth from her hands. Lights danced in front of her eyes, and she felt waves of pain shooting up into her forehead. She moaned, and her knees suddenly buckled beneath her.

"Dany," Sam whispered, barely catching her as she collapsed into his strong arms. The last thing she remembered was his arms encircling her and the warmth of his sun-hardened body pressed against hers.

Dany awoke, groggy, immediately aware of a heavy adhesive bandage across her nose. It was dark except for a small light on the nightstand beside her bed. She sensed movement rather than heard it and gasped as a bulky shadow moved from the darkness to the light.

"It's just me," Sam growled, coming over and standing above her.

Dany let out a sigh of relief, her fingers resting at the base of her throat. She felt the bed sag beneath his weight. Her eyes flew open, and she stared up at his harshly lined face. Assorted impressions hit her at once. Someone had dressed her in her black silk nightgown, and she was comfortably ensconced in her own bed. Dark smudges hovered around Sam's eyes, fatigue showing in their darkened depths. Guilt at her outburst earlier caused her to be contrite.

"How long have I been out?"

"About four hours. You went from a faint into sleep. Doc Hart said you were exhausted. He just called me about an hour ago and said you're also anemic. So that means you cool your heels for a while and take it easy and rest."

"Wonderful," she retorted, her voice thick.

"How do you feel?" he asked, managing to soften his tone.

"I'm hungry."

A slow grin appeared on his generous mouth. "Hungry?"

She glared over at him, pulling up the blanket across her breasts. "Yes, hungry. Is it a crime to be hungry after getting punched in the nose?"

His hand came forward and caressed her cheek. "Okay, okay, don't get excited. I'll go see what Martha saved from tonight's meal."

"No, I'll go down and eat. I can get up and walk."

His hand rested firmly on her naked shoulder, his fingers a burning brand to her flesh. She was all too aware of the thin spaghetti strap that held the nightgown up over her body. A blush rushed across her face, and she gave in, just to get him to leave. "Okay, I'll eat here," she muttered.

Sam smiled benignly. "That's better. You know, lady, you're worse than a flighty two-year-old filly that needs breaking." He slid his hand upward, lightly caressing her arm.

Her lips parted and she stared at him, his touch communicating much more than words possibly could. His fingers came to rest on her shoulder, his eyes a dark, turbulent gray. Her heart hammered at the base of her throat as she read the intent of his gaze. His fingers tightening against her shoulder, Sam leaned down. "Women and horses ought to be broken with love," he whispered, his breath warm against her face. "All you need is a gentle hand, Dany."

His mouth grazed her lips lightly. A deep, keening ache began within her body, and she tilted her head up hungry for further contact with his teasing, tantalizing male mouth. The fresh scent of pine intermingled with horses filled her flared nostrils. To her, it was one of the most natural scents in the world, and she relaxed as he cradled her face between his work-roughened hands. His mouth moved insistently against her lips, tasting them with delicious slowness. Instinctively she curved her arm around his neck, desiring more of what he offered.

A low groan emitted from him. "God, Dany, I need you," he murmured thickly against her ear.

She pulled away from him, reluctant to end the contact. "You're right," she admitted unsteadily. "A gentle hand and a kind word are all anyone needs." She had not meant for it to sound bitter, but it came out that way.

Sam slowly rose, an unreadable expression dropping over his face. "You need it, too, Dany," he reminded her darkly.

Desperate at the turn of the conversation, Dany cast about for anything to break the last of the heady spell. "Who put me in my nightgown?" she demanded peevishly.

He studied her for long seconds before answering. "Don't look so worried. Martha shooed us out of the room. She said it wouldn't be proper to have a bunch of gaping fools around when she dressed you. I'll be back in a few minutes with your dinner."

Dany scrunched down between the covers, groaning to herself. She shut her eyes tightly, embarrassed by the entire incident. Unconsciously, she touched her lips, aware that the strength of Sam's mouth had acted like a brand upon her. It shouldn't have happened. Not now. Unable to vent her fear and anxiety at Sam, she turned it upon Altair. "Damn you," she breathed softly. It was going to be the last time the stallion injured her, she promised. Tomorrow morning, Altair was going to start to like water... or else.

She ate ravenously, occasionally flinging a distrustful look in Sam's direction as he sat opposite her on a chair in the corner of the room. He got up, pouring himself more coffee and refilling her china cup.

"You know, you need fresh air, sunshine and some good ranch food in that body of yours to help get you back on your feet. I want you to take a week off and just rest, Dany. I can ride Altair enough to keep him in condition. I need you at your best. Not your worst."

She put the cup down, her eyes narrowing with frustration. "I run my own life, Sam Reese. How many times do I have to repeat that sentence? Tomorrow morning I'm going to begin to retrain Altair."

"You will not. Doctor Hart said you're this close to folding." He held up two fingers that were barely a quarter of an inch apart. "Quit pushing yourself. You have a roof over your head, money coming in and a job."

"Yes, and a tyrant for a boss. No thanks. I'll fulfill my bargain and leave your wonderful services as soon as possible."

He shook his head, sipping the coffee slowly. "Your compliments aren't going to get you anywhere, so quit throwing the barbs. I've been stung by a lot worse, believe me. You're exhausted, very close to a broken nose and you need to relax."

Dany bowed her head, her black hair providing a curtain between them. Deep inside she knew that he was right. There was no way that she could ride for at least a week; the jarring effect would do nothing but aggravate her nose. "You're right," she admitted quietly.

She heard him rise and looked up in his direction. His face showed his own tiredness and worry as he leaned over, taking the tray from her lap. "You got some sense after all," he murmured. "I'll look in on you tomorrow sometime. Take one of those pills the doctor left for you before you go to sleep."

She frowned, watching him walk slowly toward the door. "Don't do me any favors, Sam. You don't have to keep a check on me each day. I won't run away."

His eyes flared briefly with anger. "If I want to see how you're feeling tomorrow, I'll come. It has nothing to do with our business agreement. Understand?"

Dany opened her mouth and then shut it, glaring at him until he closed the door after him. Taking the glass of water, she placed the pill in her mouth. Shutting off the lamp, she snuggled back into bed. If it was a sleeping pill, it wasn't working. She lay there in darkness staring up at the ceiling, thinking of Sam and how he affected her.

Five

———

It was well past noon, and Dany waited nervously for Sam to come and visit her as he had promised. Martha had come up earlier, bearing a bowl of rich chicken soup and a slice of thickly crusted homemade bread. She nibbled at it, occasionally glancing up at the oak door, waiting for him to appear. Sighing deeply, she reprimanded herself and listened to music from the stereo, curling up on the sofa to read a novel. The nourishing hot soup and bread lulled her to sleep, and the book dropped from her hand, her head lolling against the overstuffed pillows on the sofa arm.

LINDSAY McKENNA 69

The scent of pine entered her nostrils, and she stirred slowly, her black hair in disarray about her shoulders. Sam finished tucking a blanket in around her body and was rising as she barely opened her eyes. "Oh," she murmured groggily, "I must have fallen asleep...."

"Keep on sleeping, lady. I just came in to check on you," he whispered, picking up his jacket and throwing it over his broad shoulder.

She was warm, drowsy and content. The husky concern in his voice was a healing balm, and she closed her eyes once again.

It was near evening when Sam gently shook her awake. A flicker of genuine concern crossed his rugged face as he sat down opposite her, folding his hands across his knees. Dany sat up, stiff from being in one position for so many hours.

"Do you realize you have two black eyes?" Sam asked, a grin beginning to appear on his mouth.

Her eyes widened and she gazed across the distance at him. "I do?"

"You look like a raccoon with a mask."

She frowned, slowly got to her feet, and put the blanket on the arm of the sofa. "What time is it?"

"Nearly six. Martha was getting worried about you sleeping so long, so I told her I'd come up and—"

"Check on me," she finished.

"Do you mind?"

"I'm not used to being looked after." She ran her fingers through her rich dark hair and caught a wistful look on his upturned face. Right now the room was comfortable with his presence, and it made her feel at home. It struck her that it seemed so natural—as if they always sat down at the end of each day to discuss little things together. She frowned, noting that he still wore a chambray shirt that was splattered with mud.

"What did you do today to get so dirty?"

"Put up fence posts on the western range. That herd of cattle we brought down from there yesterday had broke through it. Guess they thought the grass was greener on the other side."

"They're worse than horses," she muttered.

"Look, I won't stay," he said, rising. "Do you feel up to joining me downstairs for dinner tonight?"

"Of course," she said readily.

"I'll see you downstairs in half an hour then. Wear something comfortable. We don't get dressed up like you Easterners do."

After dinner, he guided her into the library where a fire was roaring in the adobe brick fireplace. He handed her a snifter of apricot brandy, and she thanked him, lounging on the sofa in front of the fire. The room was filled with trophy racks of elk, white tail, bighorn and bear. "Shot by my father and grandfather," he offered in way of explanation.

She looked at him down the length of the couch where he sat, freshly showered in a long-sleeve white shirt and blue jeans. She studied him curiously as the dancing shadows contrasted against the weathered planes of his face. She swirled the contents of brandy, inhaling its sweet fragrance.

"You're not a hunter?" she inquired.

"No. I'm environmentally inclined, Dany. We have bald eagles and condors up here on our ranch, and I'd like to keep them around."

"Condors?"

"Yes, largest birds on earth. They're from the vulture family. Maybe when you're feeling better, we'll take a two-day pack trip into the high country and I'll show you a pair of them. They should be nesting by now."

"I'm glad you didn't kill these poor stuffed animals," she confessed.

It was his turn to study her. "Oh?"

"I would have thought less of you," she admitted softly. "I don't believe in killing for killing's sake. To eat, yes. But look at that lovely elk.

Wouldn't he look majestic traversing your land? I'd love to catch a look at him on some early morning ride with his cows." She gave him a shy glance. "Don't mind me, I get carried away with my idealism."

"Who said it was idealism?"

Dany sipped the brandy. "Jean always accused me of being a dreamer of sorts." She gave an embarrassed laugh. "My idea of entertainment was to go to a movie and escape the real world for an hour or two. Silly, isn't it?"

"Not at all. We all have our escapes. I find mine by riding a horse and packing for three or four days into the interior."

The silence grew between them, the fire popping and crackling enjoyably in the background. "I thought I had responsibility," she said quietly. "But from the looks of things, you have a ranch and several other businesses to run."

Sam shrugged, finishing the contents of his snifter and getting up. He lounged his body against the mantel, watching her. "I grew up in it, Dany. By the time my father died, I had learned to run the entire operation."

"Did you want to?"

"What? Run the family business?" He allowed a partial smile to touch his mouth. "You've got an interesting insight into people. Probably why you're such a good horse trainer,'' he complimented. ''Yes and no, to answer your question. At heart, I'm just an ordinary cowpoke who loves the land and the animals. I'd trade the other three companies away and just keep the ranch if I could. Money doesn't mean that much to me in one sense. I'm happier with the earth in my hands and special people to fill the rest of my life.''

She colored in a pretty blush, catching the inference of his last huskily spoken words. She wanted to change the subject and remove the emphasis of his gaze upon her. Once again, she felt impelled to open up to him, but she remembered yesterday's encounter and tried to deflect the conversation.

''Did you notice that I had a snaffle in Altair's mouth?'' she asked.

''Yes, I did. I suppose you used your beautiful feminine wiles to persuade him to carry it.''

''First time I've heard of molasses being used to get a man to do something for you,'' she taunted dryly, grinning.

Sam returned the smile. ''Touché. Did he give you much of a problem?''

"No. He mouthed it at first, and after I got on him, I diverted his attention by doing some figure eights and some simple dressage maneuvers."

"You also used a standing martingale on him. Any trouble with that?"

"Not really. I purposely left it long so he wouldn't feel hindered. I think if I'd made it shorter, he would have thrown a royal fit."

"He's done that already. You're the first trainer he's had that saw his need to be able to raise and lower his neck as he wanted," he said, congratulating her.

Dany warmed beneath his praise. How different Sam was from Jean. She shuddered inwardly when she recalled how Jean would sharply criticize her continuing efforts to polish off the jumpers for him. Jean wanted a "push-button horse" to ride so that all he had to do was not fall off. She had worked longer hours as a consequence to please her critical ex-husband. Stealing a look up at Sam, Dany tried to suppress the fragile happiness that Sam seemed to be planting inside her. "Do you always give your trainers such support?" she asked.

He tipped his head, watching her lazily. "When they deserve it. Frankly, you've surprised me with the speed of your training methods. Usually it takes weeks to get a horse to adjust to new equipment being used on him. Altair was carrying that snaffle and martingale like it had always been a part of him. Sometimes, lady, I think you're a beautiful witch who has cast a spell over me and my horse.''

She managed a smile. ''If I were a powerful witch that could cast spells, then I wouldn't have ended up with a fractured nose,'' she laughed.

He frowned. ''You scared me out there this afternoon,'' he growled.

''What? Falling on my nose? This isn't the first time, you know. I've broken it twice in the last eight years.'' She grimaced. ''But I have to admit this was the most embarrassing.''

''Why?''

''The other two were at least in the line of duty,'' she complained good-naturedly. ''Once my hunter went head first down a steep bank, and the second time, I got thrown into a stone wall.''

Sam grimaced. ''You could have fooled me.''

''Luck,'' she promised, ''pure, unadulterated good luck. But—'' she carefully touched her nose ''—I don't know about this time.''

''Relax. The doc said it was badly bruised but not broken. Your luck's still holding. Give yourself a week's rest in the meantime. I gave him a ten-mile trot and canter this morning, and I'll gradually have the distance lengthened each day."

"He's in wonderful shape, Sam. You've done an excellent job of conditioning him for the circuit," she said, standing up and giving him the glass. He seemed pleased with her compliment and took her arm, leading her out of the cozy room.

"I'll make a deal with you, Dany," he said, walking her upstairs.

She was acutely aware of his fingers around her arm. It sent a tingling shiver up her limb, making her heart beat faster. "What?" she asked, looking up at him as he stopped and turned her around at her door.

"I've got one of my oldest broodmares foaling in the next five days. If you can baby-sit her, I'd feel a lot better. That way, you can get the rest you need and still get some physical exercise without overdoing it. The boys that work for me are range men and not grooms. It would take a big worry off my shoulders if you could check in on her while I'm gone."

Her brows moved downward. "Gone?"

Sam slid his hands across her shoulders, his thumb gently tracing the outline of her jaw and neck. "Yes," he answered absently, studying her upturned face intently. "Business down in San

Francisco. Board meetings and all that. I'll be back next Friday." He brushed her temple. "Maybe your black eyes will have disappeared by then."

His fingers, rough and callused, caressed her burning skin, a brand trailing fire across her cheek and throat. Her pulse leaped crazily, her heart thudding in response as his fingers tightened against her shoulders, drawing her toward him. "I'll miss you, Dany," he whispered, and his mouth touched her lips in a brief caress. His breath was warm and he smelled of pine and the outdoors. She was losing her grip on reality, his nearness creating a new, more frightening chaos within her yearning body. She made an effort to push away. "No, don't fight," he ordered huskily, and then his mouth claimed her lips, parting them, asking entrance into their moist depths.

Danielle moaned, closing her eyes, crushed against his rock-hard body, vibrantly aware of his maleness pushing insistently against her captured hips. An aching need began to uncoil deep within her lower body, and she felt the hunger for physical contact explode violently within her, leaving her legs weak.

Her lips throbbed with the intensity of his kiss, and she shakily touched them, staring wide-eyed up into Sam's face. She leaned weakly against the door, unable to speak. He reached out, his fingers sliding through her thick tresses.

"A parting gift," he offered huskily, "so you won't forget me over the next five days."

Dany leaned against the boxstall, wistfully content to watch the new bay foal rise unsteadily to her feet. The filly had been born without complications two hours earlier. During the half-hour delivery, Dany had held the mare's head and offered her pats of encouragement. Everyone seemed delighted with the new baby. It was Friday afternoon, and no matter what she did, her thoughts always returned to Sam. His one devastating kiss had shattered her soul and resurrected an aching awareness of her needs. Each night she lay awake, making comparisons between Jean and Sam. How could Sam's one kiss make up for all that she had been missing in four years of marriage? Jean had never taken time to explore, tease or arouse. But Sam ... she closed her eyes, resting her head against the gate. He had deliberately aroused her in a way that had caught her completely off guard. But it had not caught her body off guard at all. She sighed, shaking her head and sinking her hands deeply into the pockets of her jacket.

She walked over to the stud barn, finding Altair outside eating contentedly in his paddock. As soon as he saw her, he whinnied and trotted over to the fence where she stood. Dany patted him affectionately. "You miss him, too, don't you? Who would have thought I would miss him this much, Altair? All we do is fight—" she smiled secretly "—and make up. I guess that isn't all bad, is it, big boy?"

This morning had been her first ride since bumping her nose. It had turned out to be an outstanding gallop, and they had explored about six miles of hilly terrain, jumping fallen logs and brush thickets along the way. They had returned by mid-morning, dirty, spattered with mud and scraped by brambles or low-hanging twigs, but happy nonetheless. Altair nuzzled her gently, looking for the sugar cubes she inevitably carried in her pocket. She smiled, allowing him one cube.

Rain was forecast for early Saturday morning, and she waited with anticipation, having already put the plastic covering over her hard hat. Giving him one last fond pat, she ambled to the main ranch house. Tomorrow, Altair would begin his water training in earnest—no matter how many spills it took to get him to canter disinterestedly through any puddle. She had chosen a particularly low area where water was sure to collect, and felt that it wouldn't be too slippery for him to pull a tendon or ligament. Grimacing, Dany knew tomorrow would be hell on them both. Going inside, she poured herself a cup of coffee and sat at the kitchen table.

Martha looked up, her face locked in concentration as she furiously mixed a batch of bread dough. "Well, Miss Dany, how is our red horse out there?"

"He doesn't know what he's in for tomorrow morning," she answered.

Martha frowned dramatically. "Well, you just be careful, young lady! I never seen Sam so upset as when you fainted on him in the bathroom. The man was positively beside himself!"

"What?"

"Missy, that man was plumb scared out of his wits when you keeled over last week. Didn't you know that, girl?"

"Why—uh—no," she stammered, blushing fiercely.

"Well," Martha grumbled, "you'd best be extra careful on that stallion. Sam must think an awful lot of you to be that worried. He didn't leave your side from the time you fainted until you woke up some four hours later. Tried to get him to go downstairs and eat. I told him I'd stay with you . . . but he said no." She shook her gray head. "You're lucky to have a man like that, missy. I hope you appreciate him for it."

Dany got up, shocked by her admissions. Sam Reese never left her side? She set the cup down, even more disturbed, and decided to walk into the quiet living room. Her heart ached with loneliness. She didn't want to admit that she missed him during the last five days. Another part of her injured heart trembled with fear. She had just left a marriage where she thought she had been in love. It was her idealism, she surmised, getting in her way again. Jean always accused her of being a romantic who saw the world through rose-colored glasses. Worriedly, she trudged upstairs to her suite, unsure of which feeling to believe and anxious to hear Sam's voice booming throughout the house, announcing his return.

It was near ten o'clock when Danielle felt tiredness creeping up on her again. Dr. Hart had come over on Thursday and taken the bandage off her nose, warning her that she could still continue to go to bed early and sleep late, since she had borderline anemia. Her nose looked as good as new, and the bruised shadows beneath her eyes had disappeared. She pressed her fingers gently against the bridge of her nose, feeling tenderness but very little pain. As she climbed into bed around ten-thirty she heard the first thunderstorms of the evening rumbling toward the silent ranch house. Snuggling down beneath the goosedown covers, a knife of loneliness twisted in her heart. She had looked forward to seeing Sam, and she was worried about him traveling through the turbulent weather. Gratefully, her tired body gave out on her fretting mind, and she slept deeply as lightning forked across the black, roiling sky.

It was raining heavily when she got up at six o'clock the next morning and made her way down to the stud barn. She looked toward the parking area, disappointed at not seeing Sam's pickup there. He was already half a day late returning from San Francisco. The rain was biting and the wind surprisingly cold, sweeping down from Canada and dropping temperatures below normal for this time of year. It didn't matter. Altair was going to get his baptism in water today. Or fire, depending upon how he looked at it, she thought wryly.

Mounting up, she urged the red stallion out of the barn, asking him to move into a slow trot. Snorting, the thoroughbred bowed his head against the slashing rain. Dany brought down a pair of plastic goggles, protecting her eyes, but drastically limiting her vision. The cooler weather made him more energetic than usual. Altair moved out briskly under the sensitive monitoring of her hands and legs.

After a mile, she pushed him into a slow canter, his long legs eating up the distance easily. The stallion turned a dark sienna from being thoroughly wetted by the rain. They were both getting soaked to the skin, and twin jets of spray and mist shot from his flared nostrils as he continued to splash through the water that surrounded him on all sides. Dany felt moisture trickling down between her slicker and neck, realizing she would be thoroughly soaked within another half hour. His body moved fluidly beneath her, and she shouted praise into his ear, reaching forward and patting the crest of his neck.

The real test began at the end of the gray, mist-filled valley. By now, there were big puddles, and Dany felt the sorrel begin to lag and try to avoid them. She deliberately shifted her full weight, throwing the animal to the right or left so that his hooves sank into the two inches of water. They both worked hard and with total concentration for at least an hour before Dany pulled him down to a slow trot. Altair blew and snorted, his massive chest gleaming with sweat, mud and rainwater.

She shivered in the saddle, suddenly realizing that the rain had turned into huge, wet flakes of snow. To her the month of April meant spring weather. But to her dismay, the visibility deteriorated rapidly, and in just a few minutes she had trouble seeing. Altair whinnied worriedly, prancing to the left toward the towering mountains that were suddenly obscured by a thick curtain of snow pushed along with gusting winds. The flakes were partly made up of ice, and they stung Dany's face. Bowing her head, she tried to protect herself as she urged Altair into a canter.

Another horrifying thought occurred to her: They were at eight thousand feet in the Sierras. Gradually, old stories of freak snowstorms in the Rockies came to life in her memory. The wind was howling around them, and snow was collecting in inches. Altair was frantic, tossing his head skyward and lunging against the confines of the bit, wanting to get home to the safety of his barn. Grimly, she decided that she had no choice; to allow a risky gallop in the blinding snow would invite a fall and he could break a leg. She had to fight him every inch of the way and pray to God that they didn't get lost.

Only one thought comforted her—this horse knew the way home. She allowed Altair just enough slack on the reins to sense his way toward the ranch. Her hands lost all feeling, and ice collected on Altair's muzzle and eyelashes. A series of small hills rose like gray shadows in front of them, and Dany slowed the stallion even more; the snow was now four inches deep and continuing to accumulate at a frightening rate. Luckily, the thoroughbred was a trained hunter and knew the consistency of the ground beneath his hooves. At one point, they slid sideways, but gingerly Altair collected himself and made a half leap, landing in a bank of drifting snow. Dany called encouragement to the stallion, continually patting his neck and crooning to him. She was frightened but believed in the intelligence of the horse to find the ranch.

Suddenly, Altair pitched forward and Dany was flung over his head, landing with solid impact in a mound of snow. The stallion scrambled shakily to his feet, blowing hard, his head hanging from the exertion of the trek. Dany shook her head, thankful for her hard hat, feeling a depression that had been made in the side of it. She must have struck a rock. Crawling to her knees, she reached out, picking up Altair's slippery reins. She reeled against him momentarily, blackness closing in on her, clutching at the saddle, until it passed. Oh, God, she thought dazedly, what if I don't get him home? What if he breaks a leg out here because of my stupidity? Those thoughts forced her back into the saddle. She leaned forward, trying to shield herself from the screaming storm. Altair hung his head, more content to continue at a plodding walk through the knee-deep snow.

Dany gave a cry of relief as she saw the shadow of the stud barn suddenly appear before them. Slipping off Altair, she collapsed against the door, pounding on it weakly with her fist. Altair whinnied loudly, his bugling cry soaked up by the blizzard.

She felt the door give and struggled to stand as several men rushed forward.

"Dany!" Sam thundered, lifting her upward.

"Thank God," she whispered, pulling Altair within the warm barn. "Sam, Sam, you've got to look at Altair's leg. We fell ... maybe a mile from here." Her voice was weak, trembling, and she clung to him in order to remain standing.

"I'm not worried about the damn horse," he growled, forcing her around to face him. "I was worried sick about you! Are you all right?"

"Just a headache." Her teeth were chattering.

Sam handed the reins over to Jake. "Get him rubbed down. I'll come out later and check his legs."

"Right, boss."

"Can you walk?" he demanded.

Dany removed the goggles and hard hat, her fingers nerveless. They dropped to the floor, and she bent to pick them up. "Give me a moment," she whispered thickly. "My hands, Sam. I can't feel a thing."

"Leave that gear. Jake will bring it in later. Come on, let's get you inside and get these wet clothes off you."

Her black hair had become unknotted during the fall and hung in thick, wet ropes about her shoulders. Martha brought blankets up to her room and peppermint tea laced with hundred proof whiskey. Dany shook so badly that she could barely undress herself. Her fingers seemed frostbittten, and she sat on the bed as Sam unbuttoned the rain slicker and then her blouse, pulling them impatiently off her cool skin. "I'm sorry," she murmured, her teeth chattering every few seconds.

He gave her a dark, angry look, pulling off her riding boots, sending them flying across the floor.

"Why didn't you tell Martha where you had gone?"

She gave him a blank stare. "I did—"

"God, Dany, we looked everywhere for you. The moment I got home this morning I knew the weather was going to turn sour. Martha said you went out to get Altair used to the water. How far did you go?"

She shivered convulsively as he jerked a heavy woolen blanket around her skimpily clad form and then helped her to the bathroom. "I—I think you call it the Bluff."

He groaned, shaking his head. "That's nearly thirteen miles away. Are you telling me you came all the way back through that?" he asked disbelievingly, making her sit on a stool while he turned on the faucets to the bathtub.

Dany closed her eyes, trembling uncontrollably now. "Y—yes. Sam . . . I'm so—so cold," she whispered.

He straightened up and put his hands on his hips. "I'll get Martha to help you," he said gruffly.

As the feeling started coming back to her fingers, she felt like crying. Martha's tough exterior melted as she continued to dip Dany's blue fingers back into the water. "This is the only way,

Dany. I'm sorry it hurts so much. We caught it just in time. Why, if you'd gone fifteen or twenty minutes longer, you might have lost them. You'll feel better soon. Here, have another drink of this tea. That'll warm your innards up.''

Dany peeked warily up at Sam as he reentered the room after she had managed to dry off with Martha's help. She had found a long flannel nightgown and gotten it over her head, wanting nothing more than the warmth that the bed offered. Martha hurried down to the kitchen to warm up some beef broth.

"How's Altair?" she squeaked, her throat still feeling constricted.

"He'll be fine. He came out of this mess a lot better than you did." Sam shook his head, pulling a chair up to the bed. "Lady, you get in more trouble than a yearling colt does, you know that?"

"Ever since I came west, Sam, I've been nothing more than a liability. Maybe you ought to let me go back home—back East where—"

He growled, "This is your home for now."

She looked at him sharply. "You mean you're still going to force me to show Altair?"

"Do I have a choice?" he asked dryly. "I have to get my money back from all the medical bills you're incurring." He stared at her. "Are you always so accident-prone, Dany?"

"Normally, no."

"It wasn't your fault, really. How could you know that at this time of year we get freak blizzards?" He reached out, capturing her hand. "I went crazy trying to find you, Dany. I had seven men out on horseback searching for you until the snow started. And we had to come in. I couldn't afford to lose someone else to this damn storm."

"I need an easterner's survival guide to the West, Sam," she muttered, completely shaken by his gesture.

"Starting tomorrow, I intend to give you a short course in it, believe me," he answered grimly. "How's your head and nose feel?"

"I've got a slight headache is all. My nose survived fine," she admitted, feeling the warmth of his presence freeing her at last from the fear that had shadowed her trek home to the barn. "I just wonder if my stay here is going to continue to be so eventful."

Sam groaned, getting to his feet. "I hope not."

"Sam, you should have seen Altair," she began. "He went through all kinds of water situations! He balked a little at first, but gradually he was going through them like a champ. He trusted me enough to let me guide him through them. And you should have seen him on the way home! He's so surefooted. I'll tell you, I'm not going to worry about riding that horse in a muddy eventing field. He's the kind that will fall on his nose or hind-quarters to get up and push on. He's simply magnificent."

Sam rested his hands loosely on his hips, enjoying her enthusiasm. "Dany, you damn near got killed out there less than two hours ago and now you're bubbling about that stallion." He sighed. "Well, I guess I should have known better. But it proves me out—you are a rider as well as a trainer."

Six

"**Y**ou didn't hear what I asked you at the kitchen table downstairs earlier. I wanted to take you into Placerville at first opportunity and get you some Western boots, a hat and wrangling jeans. Since the doc has put your work duties on a thirty-day suspension, I thought you might let me introduce you to how a rancher makes a living."

There was a hint of excitement in Sam's voice, and Dany smiled. She had been resting up for two days now, and Sam's enthusiasm was catching. "You mean you're going to make a cowgirl out of me?"

Sam laughed. "Hardly. With your past accident record, I think it best you sit astride a good quarter horse and just watch. We'll be taking the main herd up to high pasture very shortly. It's an eight-day trek into the heart of the Sierras. Juan will be bringing the chuckwagon along, and we'll be eating and sleeping out under the stars. How about it?"

A tremor of excitement coursed through her, and she sat up a little straighter. "But what about Altair? Who will exercise him?"

"He'll be my personal riding horse on the trip."

The shock was apparent in her expression, and Sam provided an explanation.

"Dany, long before he ever became an eventing horse, he was a cow horse. Remember?"

She laughed. "I don't know of another eventer who has such a background except for Nautilus."

Sam rose, smiling. "Wait till you see him work. I might even let you climb aboard and cut a cow or two on him. It's an experience you'll never forget."

Dany stood, walking at his shoulder until they came to the door separating the suites. "It sounds wonderful, Sam. I don't know how good I am at camping because I've never done it before."

"No Girl Scout training?" he teased warmly, looking down at her.

She grinned. "None. I think I'll be a liability."

"Never," he whispered, reaching out and caressing her pale cheek.

Dany felt the roughness of his fingers against her skin, and a tingle shivered through her body. He was so close. So dizzyingly masculine. She was mesmerized by the silvered fire deep within his darkening eyes as he hungrily studied her. Her lips parted and her breathing became shallow. Unconsciously, she leaned her cheek toward his hand, feeling its very fiber.

Reluctantly, he dropped his hand. "You get some rest, Dany," he ordered thickly. "We'll talk more of this tonight at dinner."

She stood there awkwardly, feeling as if the sun had suddenly left the sky. She closed the door quietly, walking thoughtfully back to the couch. He could have kissed her then, just as he had outside her door before he had left for San Francisco. Touching her lips, she found herself wanting him to take her into his arms again. The admission startled her. Looking at her watch, she realized that it would be five hours before she saw him again. And somehow, that was an excruciatingly long time to wait for his return.

* * *

It was well past eight that evening when Sam entered through the kitchen, carefully placing his muddy boots outside the door. Dany had shared dinner with Martha much earlier and was helping her clean up the dishes. She noted the tiredness in Sam's eyes; there were smudges of gray shadowing beneath each one.

"Go get cleaned up, Sam, we'll warm up your dinner."

Sam managed a small smile of gratefulness as he leaned over, placing a kiss on Martha's hair. "Thanks. I'm sorry I'm late."

Dany dried her hands on the towel, leaning against the draining board. "Did you have problems, Sam?"

"Yes. But I'll tell you more about it later." He glanced over his shoulder at the small table. "Will you join me while I eat dinner?" he asked.

Dany colored. Martha raised one eyebrow, watching her expectantly. "Well—yes, if you want...."

Martha had gone off to bed, and Dany had just finished setting the table when Sam appeared silently at the door.

"Smells delicious," he said, sitting down.

"I'll bet you're starved," she said, placing the steaming portion of lamb's ribs on the blue and white porcelain plate.

"Beyond starvation," he promised fervently. "Sit down," he coaxed. "I can wait on myself."

"Let me," she protested. "Martha says you fend too well for yourself. So sit there and I'll bring over the mashed potatoes and peas."

A lulling warmth settled pleasantly over the kitchen as she served the vegetables. There was something elemental and relaxing in sharing dinner. Without another word, Sam dug hungrily into the food. For the next fifteen minutes, very few words were traded, while Dany fussed over the dishes and made a new pot of coffee. Standing at the sink, she stole a glance over at him. His hair was dark and gleamed wetly from the recent shower. He had traded the dirty chambray shirt and jeans for a clean pair of jeans and a long-sleeved white shirt. She marveled at the contrast between the dark hair on the back of his hands and the cotton material. He glanced up, wiping his mouth with the napkin.

"Delicious," he murmured.

Dany filled his ceramic mug with coffee. "Thank Martha. All I did was volunteer to peel the potatoes."

"Food cooked with love always tastes better," he persisted. "Let's have our coffee in the study."

She trailed behind, a cup balanced between her hands. Sam motioned for her to sit on the couch facing the blazing fireplace. Curling up comfortably on it, Dany acknowledged that the intimacy of the atmosphere was inducing her to relax. Sam leaned his tall body up against the mantel, sipping his coffee.

"You looked right at home in the kitchen," he commented, a hint of mirth in his low-pitched voice.

"I love to cook," she confided. "And I haven't had a chance to do much of it in the last few years." She gave an embarrassed shrug. "In my case, cooking helps me relax after a long day of fighting with headstrong young colts who think they know more than I do."

"I guess that for you, kitchen work isn't a drudgery that some women feel it is."

Dany laughed fully. "After shoveling and mucking out stalls for three-quarters of my life, Sam Reese, you *know* kitchen work is preferable!"

He laughed. "Come on, you have to agree that there's something therapeutic about cleaning out stalls. Admit it."

"Oh, you'll get no argument there. I like stretching my muscles and working up a sweat." She wrinkled her nose. "Not very feminine, huh?"

He shrugged. "I don't like women who are lazy. I enjoy someone who relishes hard physical labor as much as I do. I like sharing the beauty of this place with someone who can stand and watch the sun rise over the Sierras or sit on a rainy afternoon and listen to the rain fall." He smiled self-consciously, his voice vibrant with conviction and his eyes darkened with the passion behind his words.

Dany was moved by his sudden admission. She was secretly thrilled at being allowed to share some of his innermost thoughts about himself and what made him happy. And incredibly, she felt herself agreeing with his personal philosophy completely. The crystalline moment shimmered between them as they looked at one another.

Sam finished off the coffee and went to the liquor cabinet, pouring two brandies. He came over, handed her a snifter and sat down near her on the couch. Leaning back, he placed his booted feet up on the ponderosa pine coffee table in front of them and exhaled softly. "This is heaven," he murmured appreciatively.

Dany watched him, noticing the lines of tension melting from around his eyes and mouth. Did it take so little to make him tranquil? She was surprised to realize that she was just as relaxed. A fireplace, a study built of dark pine and padded with a thick orange carpet, plus a man contributed to her contentment. But it wasn't just any man. It was Sam Reese. It was an exquisite torment, she admitted hesitantly to herself; and when he was away on business, she missed him acutely. Yet, when he was near, her emotions became inexplicably confused.

Sam rolled his head to the left, barely opening his eyes, drinking in her features. "This is my favorite time of night," he confided huskily. "Good food, good drink and a good woman. What else is there?"

Her fingers followed the delicate curve of the crystal snifter, and she choked upon an unnamed emotion that his low voice had coaxed suddenly to life. He was a scant eight inches from her body and it would be so easy to reach out and touch his arm or to test her head against his broad, incredibly strong-looking shoulder. She sighed deeply, marshaling her scattered, tumultuous feelings. "I thought you wanted to talk to me further about Placerville."

His brows drew momentarily downward in unspoken pleasure for the disruption of the fragile truce between them. With a slow motion, he roused himself back into a sitting position. Placing the snifter on the coffee table, he murmured, "So I did. Have you decided to go with us on the drive?"

"Why not? If you can put up with a tenderfoot, I may as well try it."

"That's one thing I like about you, Dany. You don't let a new experience frighten you."

She managed a weak smile. "Oh, yes, I do. I find the past and experiences from it still stop me in some ways. Your initial proposal to come out here did, believe me."

He grinned ruefully. "A little friendly persuasion changed your mind, though."

"If that's your idea of friendly persuasion, I'd hate to meet you as an adversary in one of your other business ventures."

Sam nodded thoughtfully. "You're right about that. Although, I'm not unfair, I do enjoy the challenge. Those corporate businesses are a bore compared to running a ranch. Well, would you like to drive down to Placerville tomorrow morning with me? Martha wants me to pick up some dry goods for her. Maybe you can help me with that. I'm always terrible at getting the right brand or the best bargain.''

Dany smiled. "A man with your prestige and finances and you're worried Martha will swat you with that wooden spoon," she teased gently.

"Not really, Dany. I learned a long time ago that money is not the key to personal happiness. I could be dirt-farmer poor and still enjoy life."

"Until the last six years, I was dirt-farmer poor," she commented.

His disturbing gray gaze met her eyes. "And were you happy?"

Dany's heart began to beat more strongly. She licked her lips. "Yes. Yes, I was very happy. Of course, when my hunters began making strong showings on the major Grand Prix circuit, that was great, too."

"And then what happened?" he inquired huskily. "When I look in your blue eyes I see a terrible anguish, Dany. You aren't happy now. What will it take to erase that pain?"

Her throat constricted with tears, and she tore her gaze from him. His concern was evident by the compassionate glint in his eyes. How much harder this was to handle than Jean's acid retorts. Sam's way did not allow her to flippantly disregard his curiosity. Compressing her lips, she forced the words out, hoping to hide the strain of feeling behind them. "As I said before, the divorce is still too fresh."

Sam shook his head and reached out, gently guiding her chin toward him until their eyes met. "No, lady. There's more than that. You're so incredibly transparent. I watch the color of your eyes change. I see a shadow in there. It goes deeper than a divorce, Dany. There's a hurt..." He groped to find the correct words.

His fingers were like a branding iron to her flesh, and she sought to escape his touch. Dany fled off the couch, setting the snifter down more loudly than she intended on the table. Walking to the fireplace, she stopped, defensively folding her arms against her breasts. Why was he able to get beyond her walls that were meant to keep people out of her private anguish? An impulsive urge to confide in him burgeoned, but she checked the desire out of long habit. She'd been injured once by her innate honesty in a relationship. She had always been truthful with Jean, and where did it get her? *Nowhere,* a bitter voice shrilled warningly inside her head. The trust that she used to have had been utterly destroyed, and it made it that much harder to trust again.

"Just because you've forced me to honor a contract signed by my ex-husband doesn't give you the right to question me personally," she flung back heatedly.

Sam rose, his eyes narrowing. "No, it doesn't," he agreed. He hooked his thumbs in his belt, standing there like a bulwark of undeniable strength. "Why won't you allow anyone close to you, Dany? Are you afraid to give even a small piece of yourself to another human being? Is the cost that great to you?"

Her azure eyes widened. "Stop it!" she cried harshly. "You have no right—"

In one fluid, unbroken motion, Sam was there at her side. She tried to back away, but his hands upon her shoulders gently imprisoned her. A small cry broke from her lips as she tried to shake off his hold. His fingers tightened until she stood trembling within his grasp. His face was inches away from her own, and she felt the moistness of his breath against her hair and cheek.

"I want the right to know you, Dany," he whispered huskily. "Look at me! Why are you so afraid to meet someone's eyes?" His fingers captured her chin, forcing her to look up into his pewter gray gaze.

Her heart pounded without respite in her chest, and she gasped for breath. He was too close! She had to escape the virile masculinity that threatened to overwhelm her senses. The color of his eyes darkened to slate, and he released her chin, his fingers feather light, caressing the length of her clean jaw and slender throat.

"There," he whispered, "that's better. My wild, injured filly. So afraid of a man's hands. You flinch every time I touch you. I won't hurt you, Dany. I only want to make you happy," he murmured thickly.

Her lips parted as his mouth descended gently upon her own. He tasted, touched and outlined her lips with quivering tenderness, asking entrance, but not demanding it. A soft moan vibrated within her throat, and she tried to pull away, deluged by a tidal wave of desire. Sam's hand pressed insistently against her back, pulling her firmly against his hard body. Her heart cried for the protection and gentleness he offered. His tongue traced her lips once again, teasing, enticing. Her senses reeled, plunging headlong down an endless corridor. The pressure of his mouth increased and instinctively she melted against him, a supple willow, within his masterful embrace. A hundred careening sensations exploded within her as his tongue entwined with hers. She was aware of the roughness of his skin against her cheek, the heady masculine smell, the kneading, gentling stroke of his fingers against the length of her spine. Slowly, ever so slowly, he drew away from her wet, throbbing lips. His eyes were a fiery silver-gray, a hungry shadow within them that momentarily frightened her. Gradually, he helped her regain her balance, holding her as if she were a fragile crystal ornament within his arms.

Dany could not tear her gaze from his rugged face. Her nostrils flared as she experienced an overwhelming sensation of attraction to him. She was trembling outwardly, and she could feel him tightly controlling his own quivering need for her. Tears welled up into her eyes, quickly streaking her flushed cheeks. Sam frowned, taking his fingers and caressing her skin.

"Don't . . ." she protested weakly, "don't Sam. I—I can't take this," she croaked. "Not yet . . ."

His eyes grew troubled and he frowned, carefully cradling her chin. "Honey, I would never do anything to hurt you. I wanted to show you that sharing something didn't mean it had to be painful."

Dany took a long, unsteady breath, feeling safe within his arms. She made an effort to disengage

herself, but her legs wouldn't move. She felt
pleasantly immobilized by his strength and the
aura of magnetism that swirled around him.
"Sam," she begged, her voice scratchy, "I don't
think I could take that type of pain again." She
touched her throat, swallowing hard against a
forming lump.

He caressed her hair, his fingers trailing through
the silken tresses. "But don't you see," he coaxed
thickly. "You must start to trust in something
again. It's healing, Dany."

She slowly looked up, her eyes wide and dazed
with emotional exhaustion that the last few minutes of traumatic events had produced. "Don't
you see?" she cried with anguish in her voice. "I
don't know how to act. I'm confused. I—I
thought I knew who I was . . . what I wanted. And
it's all changed now, Sam. I feel so hopelessly
adrift . . . a cork in some endless ocean. If I don't
know myself, or trust my own perceptions of people around me yet, how can I reach out and trust
another man?"

His expression was still concerned, but his arms
slipped free of her body and his voice sounded
discouraged when he said, "How much of your
soul did he strip from you, Dany? How could
anyone do that much damage?"

Her heart felt serrated by his blunt questions. She shut her eyes tightly. "I'm sorry I don't meet your expectations. I can't overcome this distrust the way you expect me to."

"Dany," Sam began, speaking softly, "you are a woman with an incredible training record handling some of the mightiest and most powerful horseflesh in the U.S., and I guess that I've expected the same kind of toughness and resiliency in you emotionally. You are hurt far more deeply than I ever was from my marriage." He gave a slight shrug of his broad shoulders. "If I ever meet that ex of yours, I'm liable to wring his damn neck for what he's done to you, Dany."

She colored fiercely, her eyes widening at the growl in his voice. Throughout her life she had fought for every inch of ground that she had won and without help—except from her riding master. In Terrence she had found a friend, a mentor and someone she could lean on when she got tired. Sam's face held a tenderness that she had never seen before as he watched her through his half-closed eyes. A shiver of long-forgotten care enveloped her. In Sam she saw the beginning of a friendship... of trust and perhaps most importantly, honesty.

"Oh, Sam..." she whispered painfully. "I'm sorry, too... I just feel so torn inside and unsure of myself. You're strong and you seem to know exactly who you are and where you're going." She spread her hands out before her in a gesture of futility. "I don't know where I am."

He caught her right hand, capturing it firmly within his grasp. "You're here with me, honey. That's all that matters and all that counts," he urged.

Tears slid down her cheeks and she sniffed. "I know... and I'm glad. Really, I am. It's just that I'm—scared." Somehow his gesture of gentleness had allowed her the courage to confront her worst fear. She felt Sam's fingers tighten momentarily on her hand.

"Scared of what?" he coaxed softly. "I can see a shadow in your eyes, haunting you when you're alone. It can't be so bad as all that."

She reclaimed her hand, trying to dry her cheeks of the tears, and gave a helpless laugh. "Yes, it is. At least it is to me."

"Tell me," he said, setting down the snifter on the coffee table.

The silence grew in the study until there was only the crackling and popping of the fire. Dany took in a breath and exhaled slowly. "It's about riding in shows, Sam," she forced out, her voice strained. "I can't ride for you. I can train, yes ... but, please, don't ask me to ride Altair in a show." Her voice trembled and she stole a glance up at him. "Four years ago, right after I met Jean, I rode a thoroughbred called Crusader's Prince." She watched his face change when she mentioned the jumper's name and froze.

"Don't tell me—" he began.

Dany chewed on her lower lip. "Yes, I was the one." She clasped her hands in a nervous gesture in her lap. "Now do you see why I'm afraid to ride, Sam? I killed a horse, a very valuable, expensive horse, because of my own inexperience. Crusader was the top money-making jumper in the U.S., and I took him over a wall too fast. He had to be shot because of a broken leg. I miscounted the strides between jumps." She held back a sob, misery in her voice. "Oh, Sam, I can't ride Altair...it wouldn't be fair to you or to him. He's too magnificent to be killed. Don't you see?" she begged, her voice scratchy with tears.

Sam leaned forward, pulling her hands apart and holding them. "I do remember Crusader having to be destroyed, Dany. But if my memory serves me correctly the course had received record amounts of rain the night before and the ground was a muddy hell. And you weren't the only one who had problems. If I recall, one other animal had to be destroyed and two riders went to the hospital."

She was reliving the horror of the entire sequence in her mind as she had done thousands of times before. "Jean warned me not to ride the horse. He said I didn't have the experience," she said softly. "He was right, you know. I had no business doing it."

Sam snorted. "I'll just bet your ex never let you forget it, too."

"I just don't have what it takes. I don't have that fine edge of timing in critical jumps."

"The hell you don't. Look, Dany, let's treat this problem as if we were training a young horse."

"What?"

"What is the basis of training a horse to jump?"

She gave him a perplexed look. "Patience and schooling a horse over low, tightly spaced jumps at first and then working up gradually in height to larger jumps. Why?"

"If we are going to get you over your fear of riding Altair at a show, don't you think we ought to do the same thing for you? We could design some courses and gradually make them higher and

more intricate until you feel confident on Altair.
By that time, Santa Barbara will be around the
corner and you'll both be ready to take that show
by storm. What do you think about the plan?''

The roughness of his hand upon her fingers gave
her a comfort she had never experienced before.
Her heart ached with fear and unsureness. ''Sam,
I just couldn't live with myself if I destroyed another horse because of my—''

''Dammit, you listen to me! Crusader would
have died out there with another seasoned jumper
because of lousy footing. The judges should have
canceled the run and rescheduled it for another
day, but they didn't. If you can train jumpers to
become aware of their strides and realize their
takeoff point to scale a jump, you can ride in any
show successfully.'' His voice gathered conviction. ''Honey, Altair is one of the most surefooted horses you've ever had the pleasure of
meeting. That's where his questionable background as a cow horse comes in. He's used to
scrambling up and down rocky ravines chasing
wild cows or negotiating steep hills and jumping
over logs hidden by underbrush. In the years I've
owned him, he's never fallen once.'' His voice
quivered with encouragement. ''Honey, you *can*
do it. In a way, both you and Altair are scarred by

the past. But your weaknesses aren't in the same area. Together, you're complementary and strong. The stallion trusts you and that's nine-tenths of the battle right there. You know a horse will go the distance if he trusts you."

She could only stare, mesmerized by his confidence in her abilities. "Both of you trust me and I don't even trust myself," she admitted. "I can't promise you anything, Sam. This fear is so big in me that I break out in a sweat every time I think about it. That's why I fought so hard to stay in Virginia. I didn't want out of the contract because of Altair's problems. I just didn't have the courage to ride him because of the past."

"That was four years ago, Dany, and you've accumulated that much more experience under your belt." He reluctantly released her hand. "Get to bed, you're looking tired," he urged softly. "We'll get you suited up in boots and jeans tomorrow and then we'll set out for the pastures in a couple days."

Seven

The morning of the ride was crisp, cold and clear. The sun was still behind the craggy crown of the mountains as they moved their mounts down the meadow toward the milling herd in the far distance. Dany sat happily in the western saddle, snug in the beautiful sheepskin coat Sam had given her that morning. She glanced down at the new cowhide chaps that would protect her legs from bushes and brambles on the long ride, and just shook her head. She felt indescribably happy as she glanced around at the ten hands who rode in front of her. It was as if she had stepped into a time machine and had been transported magically back to the days of the Chisholm Trail. Her gaze lingered on the man heading up the group: Sam Reese. He was a tall and broad-shouldered man sitting with a born ease in the saddle. Altair, his copper coat shining like red fire, sidled and pranced beneath him. Her breath caught in her throat as she watched them move with a primal grace and beauty she had never imagined. Dany wanted to join him but she checked the childish desire. She elected to remain with Juan, instead.

Juan, the cook for the drive, sat happily ensconced on the seat of the chuck wagon. He clucked in Spanish to his team of bays and then winked over at Dany. "Your first drive, *señora?*" he shouted above all the noise.

Dany smiled. "The first! It's so exciting."

"*Sí*, it is. But also, hard work. The boss going to make you work like the rest of his hands?"

"I don't know. I told him I wanted to help and not just watch."

Juan grinned, showing the gap between his front teeth. His dark brown eyes danced with merriment. "You ride one of the best cutting horses on the ranch, *señora,* do you know that?"

Dany looked down at Bomarc in surprise. "No. You mean if a cow bolts from the herd, he'll go after it?"

"*Sí, sí.* Aye! He's a cutting devil. Only one other horse can match him and that's Altair." Juan waved his finger at Dany in good humor. "You must be a very good rider or the boss would never let you ride the gray. *Sí,* I think he wants you to work."

Dany laughed fully, feeling so many weights and shadows from the past slipping off her shoulders. It must be the beauty of the morning, the excitement-charged air and her sense of adventure that was doing it. "Looks like I have to earn my keep, doesn't it?"

Juan grinned and nodded his head emphatically. "*Sí, sí.* The gray, he likes to work drag," he explained. "It will be up to you and these other hands to establish a good speed for the herd. If a cow breaks, you must hang on and point him. He'll know what to do."

They arrived at the main holding pen almost an hour later, and Dany sensed Bomarc's anticipation, the gelding's ears twitching as the plaintive mooing of the cows, calves and steers heightened. The main gates were dragged open, and the first few Herefords drifted though to the freedom of the lush green pastures carpeted with white patches of snow. Horses snorted and pawed. Cowboys remained slouched in the saddles, the hats drawn down across their eyes. At one point, Sam swung by to check on her. She marveled at the glint in his gray eyes that gave away his excitement. He smiled, touching the brim of his hat as he cantered Altair past where she stood. Dany smiled shyly, basking in the light of his obvious care. Two Border Collies barked and snapped at the heels of several anxious cows, keeping them in line. Mud and slush were flung in all directions as a few Herefords broke from the main group. Dany watched in admiration as the chunky quarter horses spurted out after their rebellious charges, quickly bringing them back into line.

Finally, over two thousand head of cattle were loose and ambling across the floor of the valley under the careful guidance of the ranch hands. Bomarc had broken out in a light sweat, columns of steam flowing out of his flared nostrils as he airily pranced along. Dany leaned down, crooning softly to the horse, understanding his excitement because it was affecting her just as much. As the herd stretched out over half a mile, Dany lost sight of Sam. He remained near the head of the herd with several other wranglers. Juan brought up the rear with the chuck wagon, its wheels sinking deeply into the freshly plowed mud that had been churned up by the cattle. She was grateful for the sheepskin coat, because, even though the sun had risen above the peaks, the morning was still chilly.

A cow broke from the herd close to where she rode. A ranch hand gave a shout, pointing at Dany. Without any warning, Bomarc swung deftly to the right, galloping hard to thwart the escape. Dany clung to the gelding, her heart rate soaring with adrenaline. The reins remained loose in her hands to give the horse the freedom of his head as she leaned into the next move that Bomarc made. The gelding neatly sealed off the Hereford's escape by coming alongside and forcing it to return to the bulk of the herd. Dany laughed gaily, patting her horse as the gelding pranced back to his original station, blowing and snorting. "You love it!" she accused the horse.

A cowpoke cantered over, grinning. "That was some pretty fancy riding, Mrs. Daguerre," he complimented.

Dany thanked him, aware that she had been splattered by mud during the escapade.

"Looks like the boss was right. You can ride. Want to take this side of the herd?"

"Sure. Why not?"

"Good enough. If you or the gray get tired, we'll change you off for a quieter spot."

"Will this be busy?" she asked, wiping a fleck of mud off her face.

"Shortly, ma'am." He pointed toward the foothills looming in the distance. "The herd will want to turn back the minute we reach the hills. It's our job to make sure they go up there. Take that lasso on the right side of your saddle and keep it in your hand. You can use it to haze some of them back by slapping it against your chaps. The sound scares them into thinking twice before trying to break."

Dany nodded. "Got it."

"Okay, it's all yours, ma'am." He tipped the brim of his hat to her and spun his quarter horse around. Dany shook her head, elated. She suddenly caught sight of Sam as he skirted the herd, unable to tear her gaze from his form. Dany was barely able to contain her excitement as he pulled to a stop in front of her. He was smiling broadly.

"I see you got your first taste of chasing a stray."

"Yes. Mud from head to toe. But I loved it! Why didn't you tell me Bomarc was good at this?"

He turned Altair around, riding next to her. "A good rider deserves a good horse," he answered.

"I thought you wanted me safe where I couldn't hurt myself."

His gaze was warming, their legs touching briefly. Dany felt the pleasant shock of contact with his body. He squinted up toward the head of the herd, briefly watching another Hereford trying to make an unsuccessful break.

"Look, I don't want you to think I expect you to put in a twelve-hour day, Dany. It means changing mounts at least three times. Just put Bomarc back in with the others in the remuda and ask Pete for another horse." He reached over, his leather glove rough against the smoothness of her cheek. Gently, he rubbed a smudge of mud away. "You look beautiful even when you're dirty," he teased.

Her breath caught in her throat at the simple gesture. His hand was so large. Powerful. Yet, he had been gentle. She met his smiling eyes. "Dress me up and can't take me anywhere," she agreed, laughing.

"Listen, I'll see you when we break for chow at noontime. In the meantime, let Bomarc take care of you," he ordered.

Dany watched him ride off down the line, deciding that Sam was a centaur; half man, half horse. And what a magnificent team he and Altair made. She sighed, painfully aware of how happy he made he feel. Frowning momentarily, she returned to her duties, unable to probe too closely the joy simmering within her heart. She would take each day one at a time.

The sun was high by the time they broke for lunch. Now in the foothills, Dany found the chaps invaluable. The brush was knee high and occasionally thorny. Already, several wide scratches had marred the flawless surface of her chaps. She dismounted from a black quarter horse who was panting and wet with sweat. Tiredly, she leaned against the mare, her legs feeling rubbery. How many cows had they cut? God, she had lost count! Sam was right; it was hard, never-ending work. Stupid cows, she thought, lifting the hat off her head and wiping the perspiration from her brow.

Tying the black on a hastily erected rope that stretched between two towering pines, she loosened the saddle cinch to make the horse more comfortable. The snow was deeper in the shade beneath the pines, and she slogged her way through it out into the sunlight to where Juan was dishing out the chow at the chuck wagon. Picking up an aluminum plate, she waited in line. Discreetly, she looked around for Sam. Why should she be looking for him anyway? Juan filled her plate with a fragrant concoction of steaming chili and hot cornbread, handing her a cup of thick, black coffee. Dany found an old unoccupied log and sat down, decidedly starved.

"Mind if I join you?" came Sam's voice across her shoulder.

Dany lifted her chin, looking to her right. "Oh . . . no, of course not. Where were you?"

He straddled the log, facing her, and set the mug of coffee down by his foot. "Looking for me? That's a good sign," he teased genially. "I was making one last tour of the line before I came in. Trail bosses are the first up in the morning and the last to go to bed at night."

Dany returned to eating the spicy chili. It brought tears to her eyes. "You sound more like a baby-sitter. Are you pleased with the progress of the herd?" she asked.

"So far, so good," he agreed. "How are you? You look a little flushed."

She warmed at his concern. "It's the chili," she laughed. "You mean you can actually see me behind my mask of mud?"

"Nothing could hide your beauty, Dany," he returned fervently.

"Thanks! And I suppose you're going to tell me there's no shower or hot tub available tonight?"

"We'll be camping near a lake tonight. You can get a washcloth and towel from Juan and get cleaned up." He smiled recklessly. "Think you'll make it?"

"Why not? I love this. All of it," she confided.

Sam frowned momentarily, saying nothing. "You really like it?" he probed darkly.

Dany was thrown off by his sudden seriousness. "Yes, of course. How could I lie about something like this," she said gesturing around the makeshift camp.

He gave her a hesitant smile. "Let me hear you say that by the third day, lady. By tomorrow morning, you're going to be so sore I'll probably have to lift you into the saddle."

"Probably," she answered, finishing off the last of the chili. She wiped her watering eyes, giggling. "I'm not crying because I'm unhappy. This chili is something else!"

Sam nodded. "Juan's a hell of a cook. The boys would mutiny on me if he wasn't along. And you know what? I think you're more of a westerner than you realize. There aren't too many eastern women I know who could gobble down that spicy chili without complaining.''

"It's called being starved," she answered, sipping the coffee. The silence lengthened pleasantly between them, with sunlight lacing like fragile fingers of light between the evergreens. Dany relaxed within his aura of strength, suddenly content. Sam was drinking his coffee, his head turned, watching the herd of cattle in the distance. His profile was clean and rugged, reminding her of the scope of the Sierras in which they sat. Her heart mushroomed with a silent joy as she studied him. Dany found herself being mesmerized, and she tried to ignore the feelings it conjured up. Darn her romantic, blind heart. She was sitting with an incredibly handsome, masculine man in a wild, primeval country, and her imagination had run away with her once again. Grimly, she got up, fighting back the fantasies that were created by the moment and the place and the man. Sam looked back at her.

"Where you going?"

"To check on the black," she lied, feeling guilty as she saw the momentary bafflement in his eyes.

"She'll be fine," he drawled, watching her closely. "Why don't you rest for a while, Dany? We're going to be covering a lot of rugged territory this afternoon and you should sit a spell."

She shrugged unsurely. "I feel like walking a bit, Sam."

"Okay. Just watch out for rattlers. They start coming out this time of year to get a patch of sun to warm their cold bodies."

"What?" she blurted.

"Poisonous snakes," he added. "Just watch where you're stepping, Dany. Don't go wandering outside the camp."

"Sure. Of course," she murmured, shaken. Snakes. She hated snakes. Taking the plate back to Juan, she washed her utensils and dried them off. On her way to the horses, she kept her head down, watching for anything that might resemble a snake.

By eight that evening, Dany wasn't sure she could extricate herself from the saddle. She was used to riding, but not this type where she was jerked from side to side at a moment's notice. Her third horse of the day, a chestnut, appeared tired, and she spent extra time rubbing her charge down as the men began to come in and wait in line for their supper. Resting momentarily against the gelding, Dany closed her eyes, aware of the strong scent of sweat surrounding them. A hand slid across her shoulder and she gave a small gasp.

Sam's worried face hovered above her in the fading light. "You all right?" he asked.

Dany inhaled deeply, resting against the chestnut once again. "You scared me to death," she whispered.

He removed his hand somewhat reluctantly. "Sorry. I thought you were feeling faint or something. Come on over by the campfire, I think it's time you sat down and rested awhile," he urged gently.

Dany made no move to step away as his arm encircled her waist. Gratefully, she leaned against his seemingly tireless body. He had been raised in this country and toughened by it. She was a newcomer and felt inexplicably humbled by the majesty and power of the Sierras and the incredible demands of the drive. Cattle lowed in the distance, many of them grazing contentedly on the newly sprouted grass.

"We made good time today," Sam was saying as he guided her over to a log that sat near the fire. "Pete said you did a hell of a job."

Dany managed a tired smile, sinking to the beckoning length of the log. "Oh," she groaned, "it feels so good to sit down on something that doesn't move!"

Sam's hand rested reassuringly on her shoulder. "Stay here," he murmured. "I'll get us something to eat and then we'll sit here by the fire."

Dany was too exhausted to dispute the wisdom of his decision. The mouth-watering odor of grilled steak hung in the air, adding a bluish haze over the camp area. He joined her five minutes later on the log, and Dany forced herself to eat. Other cowboys sat around the blazing fire, murmuring, sharing stories of the day's ride and stretching out to relax. Darkness fell rapidly and the stars glimmered like dew droplets against the velvet expanse of the sky. Dany rested her arms against her thighs, cradling her chin. She had eaten heavily and now felt drowsy.

"Where does a tired cowpoke bed down around here, Sam?" she asked.

"Over there. Come on, I'll help you get settled. You look like you're going to keel over any moment."

Dany rose stiffly, excruciatingly aware of the crying ache of certain muscles. She grimaced up at Sam, who stood patiently waiting. "Are you still good for your word?" she asked.

Sam moved toward the circle of pines up on a small rise. "Sure. What do you want?"

"I think I'll need a boost into the saddle tomorrow," she confided, grinning sheepishly. "I thought I was in good shape for riding, but I guess I'm not. How many hours did we spend in the saddle today?"

"About ten. Tomorrow will be the same. We have even rougher country to get across tomorrow." He halted, taking one of the sleeping bags and unraveling it. Scooping up large handfuls of dried pine needles beneath it to make it soft, he unzipped it. "If you're too tired to wash up, just climb in. I'd advise you to sleep in your clothes until it gets warmer."

Dany looked longingly at the bed and touched her cheek, aware of how gritty it felt. "I should wash...."

"Okay. Come on, I'll take you down to the lake."

She followed numbly, sometimes stumbling and tripping on the rutted trail to the lake. Sam's form seemed to melt into the darkness in front of her. At the lake, he sat on a large boulder as she dipped the cloth into the icy waters and began washing her hands, arms and face.

"Beautiful night," he said huskily. "You ever seen a night like this back in Virginia?"

The coldness of the water revived her drowsy senses, and she blinked, looking up into the night. "No. The stars seem so close."

"Almost close enough to reach out and pick one. Like a Christmas tree ornament," he mused.

Dany slowly stood, awed by the tone of reverence in his voice. His flesh and blood were one with this land, and he was as much a part of it as it was of him. She smiled tiredly. "I think your ex-wife had to be crazy not to love this place, Sam. It's so beautiful and untamed. Like you," she murmured.

His eyes met hers in a searching stare. "Cynthia never developed an appreciation of nature." He half laughed as he rose. "Only certain things that nature made, like diamonds, gold and furs." His voice was heavy with irony.

"Everyone has their concept of what's important, Sam."

He stood quietly by her side, watching her in silence. "So, what is important to you, lady from the East Coast?" he murmured, his voice a husky, stroking quality.

Dany shivered, wildly aware of his quiet masculinity. "People. Feelings. Honesty," she admitted. "More than anything, honesty," she repeated half to herself.

"And you're ex-husband was not honest?"

Dany exhaled softly, feeling her heart wrench. "No. He—" She halted, unsure of what to say next. Her heart was hammering now at his closeness, at the longing that cried out for him from her soul.

He caressed her cheek with the back of his fingers, sending tremors of pleasure through her body. "I've studied his progress on the Grand Prix circuit, Dany. And he didn't start making it big until he married you. You were the reason for his international stardom, you know."

Dany stepped back, biting her lower lip. She hung her head, hearing the truth, aching inwardly because of it. "I was such a blind, romantic fool," she whispered rawly. Lifting her chin, she met his warming gray eyes. "Jean accused me of being an idealistic fool. And I was. I believed he loved me...." Hot tears scalded her eyes, and she turned her back to him, dashing them quickly away. Dany felt his hands settle on her arms, as he pulled her body back against his hard, unyielding body. She wanted to simply sink into his arms, to be held and protected for just a few blissful, unguarded moments.

"That's what I find so refreshing about you, Dany. Your lovely blue eyes tell me everything," he whispered against her ear, his breath warm and moist against her cheek. "Don't ever stop looking at the world through them. I watched you out here today. I saw the joy in them." He sighed heavily, his fingers tightening against her sensitized flesh. "I heard you laughing and saw the flush of pink in your cheeks when you were working with Pete. You loved what you were doing. And your laughter has affected everyone here in a positive way." He gave her a small shake as if to reinforce the point. "Don't throw such a magnificent part of yourself away, Dany, because some man lied and used you to his own calculating end. All men aren't like him."

Dany half turned, her lips parted, as she gazed up into his features. A slight smile pulled at one corner of his mouth, and he released her from his grip. Her pulse pounded achingly at the base of her throat; she was at a loss for any reply. Instead, she could only stare wordlessly up at Sam like a child. He reached out, taming a strand of her captured hair, and tucked it behind her right ear. "Let's get back," he said thickly, "or I won't be held accountable."

* * *

The moment her head hit the pillow of pine needles beneath the sleeping bag, she sank into a healing slumber. She dreamed of Sam and his words of encouragement. And his steadying hands upon her body. She longed to feel the quivering touch of his mouth against her lips. Someone gave her a quick shake on the shoulder, and she groggily let the dreams evaporate, tucked back into a secret chamber of her heart.

"Time to wake up, *señora*," Juan called cheerfully, slipping by her and going to wake the next cowhand.

Dany moved and then let out a groan. Her body felt like one huge bruise. Birds were chirping gaily around the awakening camp as if to urge the sun to hurry up its rise. The fresh scent of pine mixed with the mouth-watering smell of bacon frying over an open fire. The odor of coffee perking was strong, and Dany looked around, searching for Sam. She heard the snort of a horse and turned to see him riding up from the herd at a lazy trot. He pulled up, calling to some of the men and giving orders. Dismounting, Sam tied Altair to the tether rope and walked over to where she stood.

"Good morning," he said, taking off his hat.

Touching her hair, which she knew must be in terrible disarray, she murmured, "Good morning."

"I think the outdoors is good for you," he commented. "You look even more beautiful this morning."

She felt the heat of a blush stealing across her throat and managed a soft laugh. "Sam Reese, you must have gotten an A in school for blarney. Look at my hair! There're pine needles in it."

He came forward, helping her sort the needles out of her hair. "You look like the earth goddess, Ceres. No, on second thought, her lovely daughter, Persephone."

Dany made a face, suppressing a giggle. She noticed that he was freshly shaven and looked equally breathtaking to her. "Just don't let the god Pluto come up with his chariot drawn by black horses and carry me down to the depths of hell," she teased in return. The last pine needle was dislodged, and she shook loose her bound hair until it spilled like sheets of water across her shoulders. Sam's normally unreadable features softened, his eyes becoming narrowed shadows of pewter gray.

"God," he breathed softly, "you ought to wear your hair down all the time, Dany."

That simple compliment began her second day of the drive. Breakfast was over by five, and they were all in the saddle by five-thirty, pushing the lazy, sluggish herd even higher into the brush-laden hills. Sam's expression was one of forlorn wistfulness as he rode off, leaving her. Dany gloried in those few parting seconds. It was as if he had reached out, invisibly kissing her lips in farewell. Sighing, she gloried in the beauty of the Sierras, the call of the mating birds and the lullaby of lowing provided by the herd.

Bomarc moved easily beneath her as she and five other cowhands continued to push, cajole and drive the end of the herd up a particularly steep, rocky incline. The temperature had risen steadily, and at first opportunity, Dany pulled the gelding to a halt and strapped the coat behind her saddle. Rolling up her sleeves she put on a pair of deer-skin gloves and took up the lasso in her right hand. Bomarc scrambled nimbly over a series of small hills, easily catching up with the reluctant herd.

The sun was nearly overhead when a Hereford with long, bent horns broke from the herd. Dany pressed her leg against Bomarc, and they scrambled down into a V-shaped ravine after the sullen Hereford. The cow, having made the trek for many years, was determined to make good her escape. Instead of dodging back toward the herd, she clawed up and over the lip of the ravine, scrambling for the heavy brush and forest three hundred yards ahead.

Dany yelled encouragement to the gelding, leaning forward as the horse lunged over the top, sending a spray of rocks and dirt flying in all directions. Wind tore past her face as she guided the horse to the right side of the cow. Giving a loud yell, Dany slapped the lasso against her chaps. The sound echoed like pistol shot. The cow doggedly ran on, desperately moving for the cover of the brush.

"Damn!" she breathed angrily. She saw the low-hanging branches looming closer as Bomarc ran hard, his hoofs pounding deeply into the slushy mud and snow. She squeezed him hard, asking for one last spurt of power. The gray dove ahead of the old cow and, at the last second, leaned to the left, colliding heavily with the animal.

Dany heard someone yelling far behind her and disregarded the cry. The forest was close and they were going too fast, the cow stubbornly resisting the gelding's nudge. Leaning over, she drove the gray into the cow, taking the rope and slashing it down across the Hereford's eyes. Both horse and cow collided heavily as they jointly made a swing to the left, back toward the herd. Dany threw her weight to the right, suddenly feeling Bomarc falter, slipping in the mud and the carpet of slick pine needles. She was going down! Throwing the reins forward, Dany let go of the rope, bringing her arms up to protect her head. The ground came rushing up in a thunderous crash. She felt Bomarc's weight on her leg and heard the horse grunt heavily. Blackness rimmed her vision, but she lay perfectly still as the gelding rested momentarily against her left leg. The gray got shakily to his feet, mud dripping off his sweaty body. She didn't move, waiting for the blackness to disappear before she tried to get up.

"Dany! Dany!"

She turned groggily toward Sam's voice, watching Altair slide to a stop. Sam dismounted, running over to where she lay. "Dany..." he breathed heavily, leaning over her. "Are you—"

She gave him a silly grin. "I'm okay," she muttered.

His eyes broadcast his undisguised concern as he cradled her head and shoulders against his body. She glanced down at her muddy arms and legs and shook with silent laughter. Sam looked down at her strangely, undecided as to her condition.

"I'm okay," she managed between giggles. "Oh, God, I must look like the original mud pie!"

Sam managed an unsteady smile as he gently squeezed her arms and legs to make sure nothing was broken. Dany rested against his shoulder, her ear pressed against his chest. His heart was pounding thunderously, matching the cadence of her own.

"You scared the hell out of me," he growled. "Didn't you hear me calling you back?"

She slowly sat up. "No. That cow really wanted to escape."

"You should have let her go, Dany," he remonstrated, getting to his feet. "You could have hurt yourself badly in those woods. Look at those low-hanging branches," he ordered, his voice taking on a sterner note.

Properly chastised, Dany said, "I'm sorry. I didn't think."

Handling her as if she were fragile cargo, he helped her stand, seemingly afraid to release his protective hold. Reluctantly, Sam withdrew his support and rested his hands against her hips. "Better get back to the wagon and get a change of clothes," he suggested.

She nodded, moving over to where her horse stood. Running her hands down each of Bomarc's legs, she checked for injuries. Finding none, she finally stood up. Sam had mounted, scowling. Flipping the reins over the gray's head, Dany swung back into the saddle, joining him. "What's the matter?" she asked.

"You take too many chances," he growled.

"Me?" And then she smiled impishly. "Isn't that what you're trying to get me to do?"

He grinned hesitantly. "Lady, if this kind of ground doesn't faze you, then we won't have much of a problem getting you confident to ride."

"I don't know which is worse: taking a chance riding in a show or taking a chance on men," she muttered.

Sam laughed. "Sometimes one isn't much safer than the other," he commented.

"Oh, yes, it is. I can always mend a broken bone or a torn muscle. You never heal a wound to the heart," Dany murmured.

He regarded her darkly. "You can," he said, "with time."

Eight

By the end of the second day, the first plateau of hills had been scaled. Dany stood by a stream, admiring the setting sun as it spread its reddish rays over the warming land. The temperature had risen all day, and by nightfall there wasn't a cowhand who hadn't rolled up his long-sleeved shirt. Men and horses had sweated heavily all afternoon with water being consumed at a phenomenal rate. Juan had just set up the camp and a fire crackled pleasantly in the background. Someone had taken out a harmonica, and the forlorn tune wafted like a ghostly melody between the large conifers, adding to the magic of the moment.

She had discovered a stream and washed her hair less than an hour ago. It hung in dark, thick sheets about her shoulders. Taking a washcloth, she scrubbed herself free of grime. Bomarc stood patiently while she put him in the stream, washing the dried mud from his shoulder and flank. One of the cowhands shook his head as he rode by, and she returned the grin. She hadn't seen any of them giving their horse a bath.

Softly humming a tune, Dany had enough energy left to help Juan in preparations for the dinner. The Mexican bobbed his head, thanking her profusely. Soon, small chunks of onion, potato and carrots simmered in beef broth within the huge blackened kettle sitting over the fire. The hands were unsaddling their tired mounts and wearily waiting for their mug of steaming hot coffee.

Juan finished kneading the biscuit dough, asking Dany to roll it out on the uneven surface of the back of the chuck wagon gate. "I hear you gave old Lizzie a run for her money, *señora*."

Dany lifted the rolling pin, sprinkling more white flour on it. "Lizzie?" she laughed.

"That old boss cow. Pete said she tried to make for the brush, but you stopped her. You fell?"

She scratched her nose, unknowingly leaving a patch of flour on the tip of it. "Yes. Bomarc and I took a small spill. We got her turned back, though."

"Bravo! They said you were magnificent!" His almond eyes fairly gleamed with pride.

"Sam said I was stupid," she muttered, flattening out the dough more. "There," she murmured. Taking a plastic glass, she dipped it in flour and began to cut out the biscuits, quickly putting them on the baking sheets Juan provided.

"Who said you were stupid?" Sam rumbled from behind her.

Dany gave a start, whirling around. "Oh!" she gasped.

Sam looked down at her, unable to contain a grin. He reached over, rubbing the flour off her nose. "Are you always this messy in a kitchen?" he teased warmly.

Dany blushed scarlet and looked down, groaning. White splotches of flour decorated her arms and her jeans. "I should have worn a tablecloth like Juan," she muttered, returning his grin.

"Something, anyway. Now, getting back to your earlier comment, who said you were stupid?"

She returned to her duties. "My words, not yours," she corrected. "About chasing Lizzie back to the herd."

Sam leaned lazily against the wagon, watching her. "I didn't say that. You're new at this, Dany, and I just don't want you taking chances, that's all."

"I know. And you think you have worries now. Wait till we get to Santa Barbara."

"Are you always that reckless?" he wanted to know.

Dany shrugged her shoulders. "There's a difference between being reckless and taking a calculated risk."

"That's why Altair loves you. He's the same damn way. By the way, do you want to ride him tomorrow?"

Her eyebrows moved up. "Me?"

"Sure. Why not? You've handled Bomarc well. I don't think it's wise that I ride Altair for eight solid days. I want him to remember your touch and your cues."

She nodded, wiping her nose with the back of her hand. Why did it always itch when her fingers had something on them? "What kind of country will we be in tomorrow?"

"Rolling hills. Like the state of Virginia."

"Good! I was getting tired of all this brush," she admitted. "Have you seen my chaps? They look like they've gone through World War III already!"

He grinned, taking off his hat and running his fingers through his dark hair. "Makes you a veteran now, Dany. After dinner, I'd like to take you for a walk. How about it?"

She stopped making the biscuits, gazing up into his strong face. Perhaps it was being outdoors for two days. Or maybe it was the infectious magic of the Sierras. But she wanted to be with Sam. "Yes," she whispered, "I'd like that, Sam."

"Good." He touched her nose again. "If I didn't know better, I'd think you were born with flour on your nose," he teased as he was leaving.

The night remained warm, with a slight breeze drifting through the shadowed mountains from the west. The stars hung like sparkling crystals in the sky as they walked slowly up an unseen trail. The fragrant pine scent wafted up from the carpet of needles beneath their feet, and Dany inhaled deeply. She was acutely conscious of Sam's body only inches from her own. A silent unspoken strength exuded from him as surely as warmth did from the sun. On a purely feminine whim, she had tied a red ribbon around her thick ponytail. She felt his hand grip her elbow and steady her as they climbed to a rock outcropping.

"Sore?" he asked as they halted at the rim.

Dany nodded, scanning the darkness. "I was lucky I didn't break a leg or ankle today when Bomarc fell," she admitted.

"We both know that. You laid there and started laughing like a ten-year-old kid," he muttered.

She laughed softly, continuing up the narrowed trail ahead of him. She gingerly tested the earth before placing all her weight on each foot as they progressed. "Well, I can imagine how funny I looked drenched from head to foot in mud and pine needles!"

"That you did and I'm glad you came up laughing. Most women wouldn't."

"Most women aren't Grand Prix level trainers, either," she reminded him tartly.

His hands slid about her waist, pulling her to a stop. Dany held her breath, feeling the warmth of his leanly muscled body against her back. He pointed to the right. "And riders," he reminded her gently. "We're about ten miles across the valley from where a pair of condors make their home."

She remained still within his arms, his male scent a special, inviting fragrance to her senses. "Didn't you say they were rare?"

Sam leaned against the rock, drawing her against him. "Yes. They're on the endangered species list. We have a pair that mates and has one or two young ones every year. I've had officials from the Sierra Club come up and watch them for a month so a scientific record can be compiled on them." He sighed. "We really don't know that much about them. They're loners who stay as far away from civilization as possible."

Dany twisted her head, drinking in his troubled face. "Like you?"

He smiled absently, gazing down at her. "A loner, or staying as far away from civilization as I can?"

"Both."

"What do you think of loners?" he breathed, rubbing his cheek gently against the side of her head.

Her pulse pounded at the base of her throat. "That—" she stammered, losing her sense of equilibrium in the face of his overpowering presence, "that they are either very self-assured people or they are afraid to get involved emotionally."

"Then you're a loner by your own definition," he whispered, sliding his hand up the expanse of her arm and resting it on her shoulder.

Dany compressed her lips. "Are you accusing me of being afraid to get involved again?" she flared.

"Yes, I am, honey. I was that way for a long time after my divorce, too."

Dany stiffened, moving out of his arms. She wished for her coat now, suddenly chilled as she turned and met his shadowed gaze. "No one heals in nine months, Sam! Not if they really loved the person they left."

"You loved him, but he didn't love you?"

Pain wrung in her chest. "If you must know, yes! Please, can't we get on another subject?" she whispered in anguish. Why must he keep bringing up her dead marriage? Her mistake?

"I'm sorry, honey," he murmured.

She rubbed her arms in displeasure. "My personal life is my business, not yours."

"When I care about someone, I make it my business," he replied, his voice hardening. "Plus, I've stumbled onto some information that might upset you a great deal."

"Meaning what? You're talking in riddles."

"Did you know that your ex-husband is going to be showing at Santa Barbara, Dany?"

She heard herself inhale sharply. "What?"

Sam remained against the rock, watching the play of emotions across her face. "The show brochure came a day before we left on the drive. He's riding the favorite French candidate, named Falcon. You're going to be riding against him, Dany. I don't know how you feel toward him. I worry that you might be a little more emotional than normal, and I don't want to see you injured. It's as simple as that."

Tears pricked her eyes and she swallowed convulsively. A collision of feelings exploded within her. Jean was back! And in all of his international glory. Well, he had finally gotten what he wanted: the best Grand Prix horse in Europe to ride. And Sam...all his courting and courtesy were nothing more than to test the waters of her emotional stability to make sure his horse had a chance to win!

"How do you feel about riding against him?" Sam prodded coolly.

Gritting her teeth she snarled, "Like I feel toward you!"

"Anger isn't going to make it, Dany. Why are you upset with me?"

She tried to brush past him, but he reached out, easily capturing her shoulder. Turning her around, he pulled her close. "I asked you why," he demanded.

"All—all this care you've given me is nothing more than a show! You just wanted to make sure I was in good enough shape mentally and emotionally to ride that damn horse for you! I should have known better. Now let me go!" She tried to twist out of his grip. His fingers tightened, biting deeply into her flesh.

"Stop it!" he growled. "Dany...stop struggling!"

She found herself helplessly trapped against his rigid body. "I can't figure you out, woman," he breathed angrily, his face scant inches from her own. "One moment you're fighting me because I show you some affection. The next second you're angry because I'm concerned for your safety. What in the hell do you want from me?" he ground out.

Pinned completely against him, Dany felt his heart pounding thunderously. She made one more effort to escape from his grip. The ribbon that she had tied in her hair loosened as she twisted her head, the rich cascades falling around her shoulders, glinting like blue cobalt in the thin wash of moonlight. She felt his hand cupping her chin, drawing her face upward. Her lips parted in response as she heard him groan her name, his arms capturing her totally.

His mouth fell upon her lips in a plundering, breath-stealing kiss. This time, there was no tenderness, no gentleness. Fire erupted from her as his tongue invaded the moist recesses of her mouth, plunging her into a spiraling vortex of utter sensation. His mouth moved insistently against her lips, and suddenly, she felt his steel grip easing. Her legs would not hold her, and she leaned heavily against him.

"Dany...Dany..." he whispered roughly. His fingers moved through her hair, capturing the tresses, pulling her head back. She melted into his arms, helpless to stop him from assailing her again. Her hand had moved upward against his chest, weakly pushing him away. But this time, this time his mouth brushed her throbbing lips. He kissed away the pain, his tongue grazing the outline of her lips, tasting the sweetness of her mouth, coaxing her gently to become a partner. His hands moved caressingly up her rib cage, lingering against the fullness of her breast, making her shiver with need. The roughness of his face against her cheek, the warmth of his breath, the male hardness insistent against her hips, threw her into a cascading waterfall of flaring desire.

Gradually Dany floated back to earth, still in Sam's arms. At first she thought she was trembling. But it wasn't she. It was he. His breath was coming in gulps, and she sensed his need for her in that raw moment. She could barely stand after that shattering kiss. Touching her lips, she gazed up in wonder at him. His eyes were hooded, watching her with silvered fire deep in their recesses. Dany shivered, never more fully aware of her ability to arouse a man. She had never been kissed like this.... A small moan echoed in her throat as she began to understand for the first time how much she had missed in her hollow, one-sided marriage.

A white hot streak of panic made her suddenly stiffen. Was she in love with Sam Reese? Could love make her feel like this? Conflicting emotions raged across her widening azure eyes.

"Dany?" he asked unsteadily. His eyes spoke of a man who also could not endure an unbalanced relationship. He caressed her cheek, tenderly touching her lips. "I'm sorry, honey. I didn't mean to upset you. I damn near couldn't stop myself.... You drive a man to the edge of desire...."

Nine

For the next two days, although Dany was avoiding Sam, she felt that they were on a collision course, and it had forced her to reevaluate her life. For the first time in four years, there was a feeling of order in her life, despite the explosive chemistry between her and Sam.

On the morning of the third day, Sam gently shook her awake. "Wake up, sleepy head. We've got a special project ahead of us today. Come on, the coffee's on," he urged softly.

Perplexed and half-asleep, Dany obeyed, stumbling out of the sleeping bag. Dawn was barely edging the darkened horizon, a pastel ribbon of pink dimly outlined the craggy cliffs that surrounded them. A bird cawed somewhere in the rugged mountains, the echo continuing down the long, narrow valley. Dany tucked stray strands of hair behind her ears, shoved on her boots and joined Sam at the small fire.

"Why are we up so early?" she mumbled, accepting a mug of coffee from him.

Sam pushed the hat back on his head and pointed toward two large peaks that sat east of the camp. "We're going to scout ahead today. There's a narrow pass about half a day's ride from here that needs to be checked. Sometimes, because of blizzards and heavy snowfall, the river is too high for the cattle to swim. If that has happened, we have to use the alternative route up to the high pastures." He looked at her. "Want to go along?"

She pursed her lips, noting the twinkle in his gray eyes. A grin tugged at her mouth. "Sure. Why not?"

He sobered. "It will give us some time to talk, Dany. I think we owe it to one another." He came over, standing very close to her, stroking her blue black hair. "If you don't feel ready for this, you can back out. I'll understand."

There was uncertainty in his voice and it amazed her. Sam Reese had always seemed so sure of himself, but now she saw the vulnerability in his eyes. Her heart throbbed in her chest. ''No . . . no, I want to go,'' she whispered.

The camp was barely stirring to life as they rode out at a slow trot toward the last threshold before the pastures. The snow had melted completely, and the ground had dried up, making the footing excellent. Dany stole a glance over at Sam as they rode in silence. What was on his mind? The last two days, he seemed to be brooding about something. Her instincts told her it was about their budding relationship. She no longer tried to deny her own feelings for him: She loved him. And it was a kind of love that she had never experienced. He made her happy by just being there. It wasn't just a physical desire or attraction. It was a blending of his masculinity and her femininity on so many complementary levels.

The sun was peeking over the rim of the mountains when they set out, covering mile after mile at an easy pace. At one point, they halted and Dany tied her coat behind the saddle. She smiled over at Sam, and he nodded, his eyes smiling in return.

At noon, they stopped and unpacked the lunch Juan had made the night before. The chicken sandwich and crisp apples tasted delicious, washed down afterward by cold spring water. Sam had gotten up and loosened the cinches on both horses and then sat down on a rock beside her. He stretched his frame against the sun-heated boulder and touched her hair in silence, running the silken strands thoughtfully through his fingers. "You have the most beautiful hair," he murmured. "When I first met you, I thought you were a prim, strict school-teacher type."

She turned her eyes gravely to him. "And now, Sam?"

He smiled distantly, leaning his head back and closing his eyes. "You're like a multifaceted diamond. So many different, interesting sides," he teased.

Dany laughed softly. "If that's a compliment, I'll take it."

His hand rested on her golden-tanned forearm. "What did Jean think you were, honey?"

Her stomach knotted, her heart twisting in pain. "A trainer for his horses," she admitted finally.

"A wife? Lover? Housekeeper? What else?" he pressed.

Dany leaned back against the rock, closing her eyes. She was content with his nearness. "Sometimes housekeeper, always the teacher and, occasionally, his wife."

"Did you really love him?"

Dany cleared her throat. "At the time I thought I did. But distance has taken care of that perspective, Sam. What can I say? He was dashing, elegant and handsome. Hundreds of women were green with jealousy when we got engaged. I thought he loved me...."

Sam's fingers tightened momentarily on her arm, as if to take away the pain reflected in her voice. "In his own selfish way, he probably did."

She managed a cutting grimace. "It was his international playboy image and his knack at spending our hard-earned money that caused our divorce."

"So you put Richland on the market to pay the debts?"

The lump grew in her throat, and she barely rasped out, "Yes."

"So a homestead means a great deal to you, despite the amount of traveling you did on the East Coast?"

Dany pushed off the rock, standing above him. The wind playfully lifted strands of her hair around her shoulders. "Home means a great deal to everyone, Sam."

He barely opened his eyes, watching her. "I'm just interested in what it means to you, Dany. Not many people would sell off half their dream."

Her face contorted. "I didn't have a choice! And it has been ground into me that dreams don't come true. Or, if they do, they evaporate very quickly." She turned her back on him, walking back over to the horses. Dreams, Jean had said, were the paradise of fools. The only thing that counted was the here and now. One couldn't dream of being a Grand Prix winner. It had to be proved each time they rode. Dany pulled on the cinch, tightening it. The shadow of Sam's tall figure blocked out the sun, and he took the leather strap from her trembling fingers and finished looping it through, bringing the stirrup down. Resting his arm on the saddle, he looked down at her.

"There's nothing wrong with dreaming, Dany," he began huskily. "Ever since I was a young kid, I had dreams. Most of them have come true. Some of them have been shattered. But that doesn't stop me from trying again."

Her eyes were wide, filled with anguish as she met his gaze. "Dreams are for people who can afford them."

He smiled lazily. "Come on, let's mount up. We'll talk more on this as we ride," he urged.

They rode at a steady trot, their legs occasionally touching as they continued up the incline toward the pass. Dany finally broke the silence. "Which one of your dreams was destroyed, Sam?"

"My marriage," he admitted.

"What happened?"

"I had it in my head that one marriage in a lifetime was plenty." He grinned. "Of course, in today's market, more people are getting divorced than staying married. Cynthia and I are one of those statistics."

"Why did it happen?" Dany asked, surprised at her own need to know. Ordinarily she would never be so bold or brash to ask such a personal question. But Sam seemed to be inviting her to explore other nuances of himself.

"It was a merger of two large corporations," he admitted. "Looking back on it, I should have known better. But then, at twenty-three, I was still wet behind the ears. Especially to the ways and wiles of women. I saw Cyn at a party in San Francisco and fell hopelessly and romantically in love with her. She was a dream come true for me, so I thought. She had beauty, flawless elegance and

sophistication." A twinkle remained in his eyes.
"She also had an appetite for rich men who could
give her the baubles that went along with the territory."

"So, you married her?"

"Yes. You see, that's where I discovered the
difference between romantic love and real love.
After about a year, the passion began to fade and
she grew tired of me and the ranch. She wanted to
stay in San Francisco and I wanted to live in the
Sierras. Neither of us made much of an effort to
compromise our positions. We ended up being
married five years and living apart three of them.
Finally, she met another very rich gentleman and
asked for a divorce. I gave it to her. Now she's re-
married and is happily basking in the light of San
Francisco society."

"You sound so flip about the whole episode,"
Dany accused.

"At the time, I was anything but flip. I was
hurting just like you are. I did a lot of soul-
searching and asked myself a lot of questions, although I never allowed Cyn to destroy a part of
me—like Jean has destroyed your confidence in
your abilities as a rider. You either let that hurt,
anger and distrust go or carry Jean and the past
around with you every day."

She grimaced. "Ouch. Easier said than done," she returned dejectedly.

He pulled Altair down to a walk, giving the horses a deserved rest. "I think you were lonely, Dany, when you met Jean. People marry for that reason. And, it's not wrong to do it. But I think you've spent most of your adult life around animals and not people. He knew you were naive and manipulated the circumstances to his own best advantage. After all, marrying the best Grand Prix trainer in the U.S. was a shrewd move on his part. The loser in the game was you."

She could barely hold his gaze. "You're so damn perceptive," she rasped. "Why weren't you around when I needed a sounding board to try and figure that out myself? You're right: I spent too much time around horses and let the rest of the world slip through my fingers."

Sam wrapped the reins around the horn and rolled up the sleeves on his shirt. The wind had picked up significantly as they entered the rocky terrain of the pass, but the sun was hot. "Horses don't divorce you," he said wryly.

She laughed. It was true. Animals had never tried to trick or deceive her. Not like their human counterparts. "Somehow, I don't think a horse can give me the emotional support I'm looking for," she said.

Sam raised his eyes upward. "Thank God," he murmured.

Dany joined his rich laughter. Suddenly, she felt more at ease than ever before. The walls of the rocky pass rose on either side of them as they moved down the dusty trail. The clip-clop of hoofs striking the hardened earth echoed through the expanse. The sky was a bright, cerulean blue, and the sun struck the planes of yellow ochre stone, lending it a golden radiance. The silent camaraderie between them grew, and Dany traded a smile with him from time to time.

They rode another two miles before she picked up the sound of water in the distance. As they came around another curve the sparkling expanse of a wide river met her curious gaze. Dany dismounted, marveling at the wild, inherent beauty of the river. A waterfall roared a half a mile away, water spilling over the lip of the gorge above them. The river frothed and foamed, indicating strong currents at work beneath its sparkling surface. Sam dismounted, hanging his hat on the saddle horn. He hobbled both horses and unsaddled them. Dany slipped the bridles off their heads so that they could eat a well-earned lunch on the lush grass.

"This is incredibly beautiful," she said, awe in her tone.

"I love coming here," he murmured. He walked upstream, gauging the river with narrowed eyes.

Dany knelt down, splashing water on her face, the coolness refreshing to her hot, perspiring body. She glanced up at him, a grin on her mouth. "What I'd give for a bath! This is perfect. Look at that sandbar. There's a small inlet that's sure to be warmer than the river."

Sam turned. "Go ahead. Take one."

She got to her feet, wiping her hands on her jeans. "You mean it?"

"Sure. I'm going to walk about half a mile downstream on foot and check the crossing point. We'll give the horses a breather and let them eat while I'm gone." He grinned recklessly. "Although, it would be far more enjoyable to stay and scrub your back."

Dany colored, pulling the sleeping bag off the saddle and hunting for her towel and soap. "I'll make a point of hurrying then," she retorted.

Sam picked up his hat. "Take your time, honey. I'll be back in about forty minutes. Just watch for snakes. There's water moccasins up here, you know."

Dany groaned, distressed. "Sam! You just ruined my enthusiasm."

"Sorry. But you always have to be careful out in the wilds, Dany. I'll be back in a while."

By the time she had finished searching for snakes, Sam had disappeared around the curve of the river bank. Dany smiled eagerly as she undressed and placed the clothes on a nearby rock. The sun struck her skin, warming her deliciously. Sitting on the bank, she slid her toe into the inviting inlet. It was cool, but not icy. Well, she decided firmly, a few minutes of discomfort are better than staying dirty. She gasped as the blue green water closed about her as she dog-paddled to the sand beach until she stood in knee deep water. Soaping her body quickly, Dany scrubbed her skin until it glowed a healthy pink. Taking a quick dip, she rinsed off. Then, holding her breath, she dove under, wetting her black hair. Again, she scrubbed furiously. The breeze on her wet skin made goose pimples rise on her flesh. She rinsed her hair and took one last dip, swimming for the shore.

Scrambling out, she struggled back into the clothes. Almost immediately, she felt better.

Looking down toward the curve, she didn't see Sam returning yet. Taking advantage of the time, she lay on the fragrant grass, closing her eyes and allowing the heat of the sun to lull her to sleep.

She was startled awake by Altair's challenging scream. The red stallion reared high into the air, his hoofs pawing the air directly above her. His nostrils were flared, and the white of his eyes could be seen. A cry lodged in her throat, and Dany threw up her arm to protect her face as the stallion came down. The earth shook heavily where he landed. The stallion pawed the ground squealing savagely. She rolled away, shakily getting to her feet.

"Dany!" Sam thundered, running toward her.

Dany twisted around, confused. His face was contorted with concern as he reached out for her. His fingers bit deeply into her flesh as he nearly jerked her off her feet. She fell heavily against him as he dragged her away from the angry stallion.

Black hair swirled around her face, and she shakily pushed it away in order to see. "What happened?" she cried.

"It must be a snake," he rasped. He thrust her aside. "Stay here," he ordered.

Dany watched wide-eyed as Sam went forward. Altair had stopped pawing and stood quivering.

Sam crooned to him, moving up to where the stallion remained frozen. He took him by the halter, releasing the hobbles and leading him away from the area. After tying him to a low-hanging tree limb, Sam returned to her side.

"Want to see what got him so upset?"

She nodded, suddenly grateful for his arm about her waist. The area where she had fallen asleep was completely harrowed. The grass had been torn up in clumps by Altair's striking hoofs. And there, in the middle of the furrowed area lay the remains of a snake. Dany took a step back, gasping.

"Oh, God, Sam," she whispered tightly. "I fell asleep. He—" She glanced over at the red stallion. "Altair must have seen the snake coming toward me. . . ." She shivered, burying herself within his arms. "I could have been killed," she breathed.

Sam caressed her head, holding her tightly. "Yes. If the snake hadn't bit you, Altair might have struck you by mistake. He has a long history of hating snakes and will go to any length to kill one," he muttered grimly. "You all right, honey? God, you're shaking like a leaf. Here, let me take a look at you."

She stood trembling within the shelter of his arms as the full impact of what might have happened crashed down on her. "W-was it a poisonous snake?" she chattered.

"Yes, looks like a copperhead. Probably came down to the river looking for rodents taking a drink of water this time of day. Well, you look okay. A few grass stains on your elbow here, but otherwise, all right. How do you feel? You look pale."

Her legs were suddenly turning to jelly, and she reached out, gripping Sam's arm. "I—I don't feel very well, Sam...."

In the next instant, he had scooped her up into his arms as if she were a mere feather. Gratefully, she rested her head against his shoulder, shutting her eyes tightly. His arms were protective and strong around her body as she slid her hands around his neck, seeking his closeness. The enormity of the events shook her deeply. She could have been bitten. She could have died! Oh, God, she didn't want to die! Not now. Not realizing how much she loved Sam! A sob tore from her lips, and she clung tightly to Sam.

"Shhhh," he whispered, gently depositing her beneath a pine tree. "Everything is all right, Dany." He placed a kiss on her head, awkwardly brushing away the tears rolling down her cheeks. He knelt at her side, bringing her against his sunwarmed body and crooning wordless endearments. Dany sighed softly, feeling his heart thundering against her breasts. It seemed natural as he raised her chin, his mouth claiming her wet, salty lips with quivering tenderness, tasting them. The pressure increased as she parted her lips, allowing his exploring tongue deep into the moist depths of her mouth. A soft moan of need vibrated in her throat, and she pressed her body against him instinctively. Sam groaned, gripping her shoulder. He pulled her away, his eyes blazing with barely constrained desire.

"I want you," he whispered thickly. "God, how I need you, Dany...."

The brush with death had torn any remnants of her uncertainty and distrust away. Shyly, she reached up, caressing his weather-hardened cheek. "Love me," she sighed, "please...Sam, love me..." He kissed her tear-wet lashes, cheeks and lips in answer. With maddening slowness, he stripped the clothes from his powerfully built body. Dany reveled in the broad planes of his muscular chest, the chiseled flatness of his stomach and his long, athletic thighs. His skin was a soft golden color, his muscles rippling with breathtaking movement as he slid down beside her, his mouth capturing her lips, pulling her fiercely against him. His fingers expertly worked the buttons free, slipping the blouse off her shoulders. She trembled as he trailed a series of fiery kisses the length of her neck to the valley between her breasts. Each touch quickened her awakening desires. Her skin tightened beneath each grazing caress of his feather-light touch. His mouth teased the flesh of her taut breasts, and she gasped, arching beneath him.

She was no longer thinking, only reacting. She was a musical instrument within the hands of a master, and for the first time in years, she wanted to be an active participant in the sharing of love. His hand cupped the small of her back, lifting her upward to meet him. Her fingers dug deeply into his thickly corded shoulder muscles, breath suspended in anticipation. His entry was swift, penetrating and fiery, and a small cry broke from her lips. She buried her head momentarily against his neck, sweat grazing her cheek. Gently, ever so gently, he brought her back into rhythm with himself. The seconds of pain fled, replaced with a delicious sense of delectable euphoria. She was mindless, simply swirling into a layer of intensified pleasure never before experienced. Sam groaned, gripping her tightly, and she gloried in those moments of mutual climax. Clinging silently to his quivering body afterward, Dany rested her spent, damp form against him. Her hair spilled across his shoulder and chest like an ebony blanket as she nuzzled against his cheek. Moments, precious, delicious moments were spilled by her satiated senses.

Sam cradled her tenderly within his arms. He leaned over, smoothing away small tendrils that clung damply to her cheek. His eyes were dark with consumed passion as he stroked her hair.

"I knew it would be good," he murmured huskily, "but I never realized . . ."

Dany saw the face of a man fulfilled. No longer did the partial mask remain to hide his incredible range of emotions. There was a boyish vulnerability in his eyes as he drank in her form, and it delighted her. She ran her fingers through the silken mat of hair on his broad, powerful chest, a tremulous smile on her lips. "Oh, Sam," she whispered and then tears caught in her throat and she was unable to continue. He laughed throatily, pulling her near, burying his face within the shining mass of hair.

"You're mine," he growled fiercely. Then he sealed this promise with a long and delicious kiss.

Ten

It was dusk by the time they got back to the herd. Cowboys on horseback walked their mounts slowly around the huge circle of cattle, singing softly to settle them down for the night hours. Somewhere out on the open stretch of the oblong valley floor, the mournful tune of the harmonica brought back nostalgic moments to Dany. She rose in silence beside Sam, content to be close to him, their legs brushing often against the other. Her body remained bathed with the glow of his love-making earlier. She could only stare at him like a child who had been given the precious gift of love.

The comparison between Jean's loving and Sam's was jolting. Sam had loved her as a sharing partner in a beautiful experience. Jean had never shared anything; it had always been take—take and never give. With that knowledge, Dany began to put the pieces of her marriage into perspective. She glanced to the left, realizing that she owed it all to the man who rode at her side. Occasionally Sam would catch her wide-eyed gaze and smile, as if sharing that intimate secret with her.

Juan welcomed them back in a mixture of Spanish and English. Dany sat near the chuck wagon, ravenously consuming her meal as she watched Sam talk to his men about the day's progress on the drive. Later, as darkness fell, she noticed the horizon seeming to blaze with flashes of light. Juan muttered something in Spanish as he finished washing the rest of the tin plates. Dany got up, handing the plate to him. She tugged at the dish towel stuffed in his back pocket and began drying the stack of dishes for him.

"Is that lightning?" she asked.

"*Sí, sí.* Not good, *señora.* These cattle..." And he shook his head, keeping the rest of his thoughts to himself.

"I would think they're used to lightning," she commented, placing the dried utensils on one corner of the wagon tailgate.

"*Sí*, you would think that. But these Herefords will get restless. I think the boss will keep everyone up tonight to ride around the herd and keep them calm."

Dany noticed that more than one ranch hand was watching the horizon apprehensively where the line of thunderstorms were building. There was an unspoken tenseness building in the camp, and she hurriedly finished the drying chores and sought out Sam. She found him with his head drovers near a stand of pine. He slid his hand around her shoulder, making her feel welcome to the small knot of men.

"Juan said the thunderstorms might scare the herd, Sam."

"There's a good possibility of that," he agreed quietly. He looked up at his men. "Pete, you take five of the boys for night duty and keep those cows content. If they start to spook, send a runner back and we'll get everyone in the saddle."

"Right, Boss."

Sam steered her out of the grove and onto the open plain. The cattle looked like shadowy black shapes moving sluggishly beneath the increasing

light of the moon. Dany sensed his concern and
turned, looking up into his worried features. "Did
you expect storms on the drive?"

"Yes and no," he muttered, stroking her cheek
tenderly. "Sometimes we get bad ones at this time
of year, but I was hoping that we would get lucky
and miss them."

"No Irish blood in you for luck," she teased
fondly.

Sam smiled absently. "None," he agreed, his
eyes soft with tenderness as he gazed down at her.

"If it rains, that means that the river in the pass
will rise."

He leaned down kissing her forehead gently.
"See, you're more of a cowgirl than you realized.
Yes, if it rises any more, we won't be able to swim
the herd across. But I'm more worried about them
spooking and then running across this meadow
into the foothills." He sighed heavily. "God, that
will be a mess if that happens. It means spending
days recollecting the scattered herd, and we'll have
to destroy those with broken legs."

Dany lunged upward, tangled in her sleeping
bag. The crash of thunder was deafening. Nearby,
she heard the men shouting, the horses whinny-
ing nervously and the cattle bellowing. A bolt of
lightning ripped the belly of the sky open and

thunder growled savagely. Dany rose shakily to her feet, throwing on her boots. Juan ran around the end of the chuck wagon, his eyes wide.

"*Señora!* Quick! Get on Altair. The herd is going to break!" he shouted.

Large drops of rain plopped on the dry earth. Dany blinked, running jerkily toward the line of tied horses. Sam had given orders that they remain saddled. All she had to do was slip Altair's hackamore on him and she could leave. Her heart was pumping strongly now. Sam, where was Sam? She yelled out for him, cupping her hands to her mouth. Again, she called for him. Indecision tore at her, and she grabbed the bridle, soothing Altair. Fingers shaking, she managed to get it over the horse's head. A cacophony of harsh sounds broke simultaneously around her. She mounted, her leg barely across the stallion's back when the herd panicked. Altair plunged forward, snorting loudly.

Three blinding, brilliant bolts hit the valley floor simultaneously. A tree exploded, the sound rupturing like an artillery shell. As a dark, willful mass, the herd veered and broke blindly into the blackness and sudden downpour. A scream lodged at the back of her throat as Dany saw a wall of Herefords bearing down directly on where she stood on the frightened, rearing stallion. She froze for only a second, leaning far forward on Altair, asking him to leap into the unknown darkness beyond the wagon. She saw Juan on another horse, swallowed up almost immediately by the engulfing inkiness.

Rain fell like slashing, cutting knives. Dany threw her hand across her eyes, totally disoriented. She heard the roar of the herd behind her, the shouts of the cowboys and the earth-shaking tremors caused by the lightning, thunder and the hoofs of the crazed cattle. The earth quickly changed into mud, and Altair lengthened his giant stride, flying through the pandemonium. Dany tried to gather her scattered, shocked senses. She had to get out from in front of the stampede! If she fell—the thought of being trampled made her stomach tighten, and desperately she tried to recall the layout of the valley. Guiding Altair to the right on a slight angle, she would cut diagonally in front of the herd, and keep the distance between them!

The entire experience was foreign to her. Diving headlong into darkness and rain at full speed was sheer stupidity. It invited disaster, but she had no choice. Where was Sam? Was he safe? And Altair. Oh, God, she couldn't allow Altair to be injured. Dany increased the angle of the turn, hoping desperately to meet the safety of the tree line. She was soaked to the skin, her shirt clinging to her, water running in rivulets across her drawn face. The charging herd was much closer. Gripping the rain-slick reins tightly, Dany called out to the horse, asking him for a final effort. The stallion lunged strongly, his nostrils wide, drinking in great draughts of wind to sustain his effort.

Suddenly, they were surrounded by trees. Dany pulled Altair to a skidding stop, pine branches whipping back and cutting at her unprotected body. Her breath came in great ragged sobs as she leaned weakly against the stallion's wet mane. Herefords careened so close that she guided Altair further into the tree line for protection. As she sat huddled in the saddle, the temperature began dropping and the wind picked up in gusts. Dany shivered, her hair in long ropes about her face and shoulders. Finally, the lightning eased and the thick, inky blackness descended once more. The bulk of the herd had passed, and the shouts of the men and the bawling of cattle seemed like a distant nightmare.

The dawn crawled cautiously onto the horizon, forcing the night back inches at a time from its tenacious hold on the earth. Dany had remained mounted throughout the long night, searching for Sam. It was an impossible task. Part of the herd had been gathered at the far end of the valley, and she saw both cattle and riders wearily coming back in this direction. Dany saw Juan's dejected features brighten as she came within shouting distance. He seemed relieved, and animatedly gestured, running out to meet her.

"Señora! Señora, pronto!" he shouted.

Dany swallowed hard, kicking Altair into a gallop. She finally slid him to a stop, shakily dismounting. "What is it?" she demanded breathlessly.

"The boss, he's over on the eastern edge of the meadow. He's worried about you."

Dany touched her breast, closing her eyes. "Thank God he's safe!" she whispered fiercely.

Juan grinned broadly. *"Sí,* he's tough. He said as soon as I saw you to get you over to him."

Remounting, she tossed the cook a broad smile. "Thanks, Juan."

Some of her initial joy faded as she rode along the edge of the flatland. Cowboys were putting animals who had broken their legs during the night out of their misery. Seeing Sam made her heartbeat rise. He caught sight of her, pulling Bomarc away from the herd and meeting her halfway.

Dany pulled Altair to a stop, reaching out and touching his extended hand.

"You all right?" he asked, gripping her hand tightly.

"Yes. A little tired, that's all," she answered breathlessly. "And you?" She searched his worn face, the exhaustion from the search for the herd evident on his features.

A crooked smile crossed his mouth. "I'll live now that I know you're safe. Look, you go back and help Juan get some breakfast on. We're going to be waylaid here a day just getting the herd back together and repairing the chuck wagon."

Dany nodded, reluctant to break the touch of their fingers. "Be careful," she whispered.

Sam grinned carelessly. "Now that I got someone who cares whether or not I break my neck, I will," he responded, turning Bomarc away and heading back to the main herd.

They arrived back at the Cross Bar-U on the ninth day, tired, dirty and worn. There wasn't a horse whose head wasn't hanging from exhaustion or a cowpoke whose face didn't speak of the trouble on the trail. Dany slid off Altair, resting her head against the horse for a moment. Sam came up, sliding his arm around her shoulders.

"Honey, you get inside and take a long, hot bath," he ordered.

Dany met his gaze, forcing a small smile. "It sounds like heaven," she agreed.

"I'll see you at dinner tonight. Get some rest."

Martha welcomed her back with open arms, giving her a long hug. Shooing her upstairs, the old woman insisted upon drawing the bath water herself, clucking sympathetically over the events of the drive as Dany related them.

"Missy, you just lay there and soak," she said sternly, shaking her finger at her. "I'll bring you up a healthy lunch in about an hour."

She dozed off in the bath much to her own surprise. Martha had slipped in and out of the suite without awakening her, depositing a tray with thick beef sandwiches, potato chips and a tall, cool glass of iced lemonade on it. Still in her robe, Dany hungrily consumed the food and didn't fight the need to simply fall on the bed and sleep.

It was dark when she awoke. The warm late-spring breeze stirred in the room as Dany slowly sat up, pushing her dark hair off her face. Looking at her watch on the dresser, she saw that it was nearly eight o'clock. With a groan, she pushed off the bed and slowly dressed in a pair of burgundy slacks and a pale pink blouse.

There was a reassuring familiarity to the ranch house as she padded downstairs. She heard Sam's voice in the kitchen and walked into the well-lit room. Martha had just finished dishes and clucked at her sympathetically.

"Miss Dany, you look positively exhausted!"

Dany shrugged, peering over her shoulder at the food to be placed into the refrigerator. "I feel a lot better," she murmured.

"Come and sit down," Sam said. "Martha can get that."

Martha's mouth thinned stubbornly. "You hear Sam? Go sit down before I take a wooden paddle to you."

Dany smiled, exchanging a warm glance with Sam as she sat opposite him. He looked at her carefully, missing nothing. "You do look better," he agreed, sipping his coffee.

"I don't think my rear is ever going to be the same. Do you realize I've got saddle sores?" she said, laughing good-naturedly.

"You earned them," Sam said, suppressing a grin.

"Humph, is that all I get for my trouble?"

"Yup. That and the knowledge that you can do a hell of a good job at ranch work."

Martha placed the fragrant meal before her. "You children enjoy yourselves. I'm going to bed. This has been too much of a busy day for my eighty-year-old body."

Sam murmured good-night to her, and the silence settled like a warm cloak over the kitchen. Dany ate the barbecued chicken with relish, polishing off the mashed potatoes, corn and a salad. Sam leaned back, a pleased expression in his eyes.

"At least you're eating," he murmured. "Looks like the Sierras are good for you after all."

She wanted to say, "you're good for me," but didn't. Instead, a blush stained her cheeks in response. Even in her sleep she had dreamed of Sam loving her. Each magical touch of his fingers upon her body lingered in her mind. She stared at his work-roughened hands, amazed at the innate gentleness in them when he had loved her.

"Tomorrow morning, Dany, I'm going to have a small jump course set up for you and Altair. We've got about two weeks before the Santa Barbara show, and we might as well start building your confidence."

Her head snapped up and she met his gaze. "I suppose you're right," she whispered. Getting up, she washed off the plate and silverware, placing them in the dishwasher. Dany leaned against the draining board, her arms across her chest in a defensive gesture.

"Scared?" he inquired gently.

"Very."

"I'll be with you every step of the way, Dany."

"I know. But..."

Sam tilted his head. "What?"

She gave a shrug of defeat. "No matter how much you want to help me, Sam, in the end, I have to do it myself."

"I know that, honey. I don't expect you to win at Santa Barbara, Dany. You know that, don't you?"

"But if I do it, I'm planning on placing," she said.

Sam shook his head. "It's too soon to be that competitive, although you certainly have that quality in you. No, the main thing is to get you to feel comfortable about riding in major shows again."

Dany took a long, uneven breath. "God, I don't know, Sam. Jean is going to be there and—"

Sam walked over, standing above her. "One step at a time, Dany. I'll make damn sure he isn't around to try to wreck your confidence before you ride."

Dany waited until Sam came up to join her at the beginning of the small jump course he had erected earlier. It was nearly ten o'clock and already she could feel the coolness of the morning evaporating.

"Ready?" he asked, his voice low and soothing.

"I suppose. First, let's count the strides between jumps."

Sam remained silent as she walked the distance between each jump, mentally calculating how many strides it would take. At a certain point, the jumper had to lift off in order to make it a clean leap and not touch the rails. It was a timed event. Whoever had the least amount of faults and finished with the fastest time would be the winner. If a horse touched the jump, then he accumulated faults against his final score.

Dany was familiar with the odd names given the different and various jumps. There was the oxer, the brush and the in-and-out. Each posed a different problem for the horse and rider. The in-and-out asked the horse to be collected and well in hand because a half-stride too much would throw both the horse and rider into the second jump. The brush consisted of still bristles at the top of it, and no horse wanted it to brush its sensitive back legs.

On the Grand Prix circuit, Dany had to count strides along the two or three mile course and keep those figures in her head. One stride too many could result in disaster, and Dany was all too aware of the possibility. Because of her burgeoning feelings toward Sam and her love of the scarred red stallion, she didn't want to disappoint them. Chewing on her lip, she finished pacing the course, giving Sam a curt nod.

With Sam's help, she mounted the frisky Altair. The sorrel pawed eagerly at the ground, wanting to be released. Dany carefully wove the reins of the hackamore and snaffle between her leather-gloved fingers. Sam's hand rested reassuringly on her thigh as he looked up at her.

"Are you going to try and work with the snaffle more today?"

"A little. Right now all I want to do is remember the count," she answered, her voice taut and more brisk than she meant it to be.

"You'll do fine, honey," he soothed, stepping away.

Hard hat in place, Dany compressed her lips, then squeezed Altair. The stallion moved out easily, making large, lazy circles while she warmed him up. No hot-blooded horse, particularly an animal in peak physical condition, was ever asked to jump without properly warming up. More than one horse had been injured and pulled a ligament because he was "cold." After fifteen minutes of figure eights, circles and some light dressage movements, Dany felt the stallion become more supple and responsive.

There were eight jumps facing her when she brought Altair around and out of a final circle. Sam stood off to the right, a stopwatch in his hand. Nudging him into a controlled gallop, she mentally counted each stride to the first oxer, which was two and a half feet high. On cue from her leg, Altair lifted his front legs, his mighty hindquarters coiling like a spring and thrusting them up and over the small jump.

Each jump became a small victory for her. Finally after sailing over the eighth one without a fault she broke into a grin. Leaning down, she patted Altair enthusiastically, praising the stallion. She trotted him back to where Sam stood.

"Well?" she gasped, pulling him to a stop and dismounting.

Sam smiled. "Not a bad time and no faults. You did damn well. Both of you," he said, placing his arm around her and drawing her against his body.

Dany laughed freely, automatically slipping her arms around his waist, resting her head against his shoulder. It seemed so natural until the importance of the gesture dawned upon her. She extricated herself from his arms, and he gave her a questioning glance, but said nothing.

"Let's do it again," Sam suggested. "Each time it will get easier. How did Altair handle for you?"

"Great. He's a doll about cuing for takeoffs, and when I wanted him to slow slightly, I used the snaffle and he responded right away."

Sam took off his hat, pushing his hair back with his fingers as he eyed the stallion. "I wonder if it would be wise to show him in just the snaffle if he continues to progress at Santa Barbara."

"Don't throw too many new things my way, Sam. He's used to the pressure of the hackamore, and I think he's going to be a handful at a show. I'll probably use the hackamore on the cross-country and the snaffle for the dressage test."

"Keeping the snaffle in his mouth for the cross-country would be a wise idea."

"Yes. Tell me, how does he behave at a show?"

Sam grinned mischievously. "He talks to all the ladies."

Dany laughed. "This horse is so much like you it isn't even funny," she commented wryly.

"Oh? In what way?"

"You're all male and you're both incredibly confident. A gentle hand and a soft voice will get more out of you than a crop or spurs."

His eyes darkened. "Maybe I am a little like the stallion," he agreed. "But not just any woman's touch would do," he murmured huskily. "Just yours." He reached over, patting Altair. "See? He's responding beautifully to your voice and hands. You're an unbeatable combination."

Dany colored beneath his loving gaze and gathered up the reins, remounting. She got positively weak in the knees every time he spoke to her in that tone of voice. Sam Reese could get to be an intoxicating habit.

By noon they halted. Sam helped her cool out Altair and then wash him in the shower at the end of the barn. It was sharing the little things with Sam that made her heart sing with newfound joy. It brought back painful memories of times when Jean would idly sit back while she worked, talking about his latest win or who he was going to be competing against at the next show. He never offered to help bathe her charges, walk them out or wrap their slender, valuable legs after a grueling training session.

They stood in the stall, both of them kneeling down by Altair's front legs. Sam passed her the thick cotton matting beneath Altair's belly, and Dany carefully wrapped Altair's foreleg. Sam covered her fingers, and she gently disengaged them while he held the cotton in place. Picking up the elastic bandage, Dany expertly wrapped it around the cotton. She caught Sam watching her with a tender flame of interest in his gray eyes.

"You make everything fun," she admitted, beginning to wrap the second leg.

"Must be the company I've been keeping lately."

She laughed softly. "I feel like I've got an unbeatable team working beside me and I can do nothing but win."

He captured her fingers for a moment against the horse's leg. "You're already a winner, Dany. You just don't realize it yet."

She moved to Altair's hind legs, unable to meet his gaze, swallowing the tears lodged in her throat. Sam got up and leaned against the boxstall as she began wrapping the fourth leg.

"You have any family, Dany?" he asked softly.

Altair snorted, pulling a mouthful of hay from the net suspended in the corner of the stall. Dany changed position and completed the wrap. She got to her feet, dusting the fresh straw off from her breeches. "Yes, my mother."

"She lives back East?"

"Yes." Dany brushed strands of hair away from her temple, gathering up the accessories and placing them into a small tack box.

"What about your father?"

Dany remained silent, and she nervously moved from the stall, letting him slide the door shut. He finally cornered her in the tack room. Grasping her arm, he forced her to turn and face him. "I'm stepping on a sore spot with you, Dany. Tell me it's none of my business and I won't ask you any more questions," he murmured.

His closeness always brought out the strength that she needed to break through yet another old barrier. "No, Sam, I'll tell you." She tossed the cloth down on the saddle that she was going to clean. "My mother really doesn't care for the occupation I'm in, to tell you the truth. My dad— well, he was an alcoholic and left us to fend for ourselves when I was eleven years old." She gave a small shrug. "Actually, we were both glad to see him go. He used to beat up on Mom . . ."

"Did he hurt you?"

"No. Not physically."

"Just emotionally and mentally," Sam growled.

"A lot of people have had it rougher than me," she reminded him. She picked up the saddle soap, turning it slowly in her hands. "Maybe that's why I didn't marry until I was twenty-four, Sam. I didn't want the unhappiness I saw in my mother's marriage. She always said she got married too young and I should wait.... Well, I did and I still made a lousy choice."

"Not really," Sam answered softly, catching her unhappy gaze. "You didn't marry an alcoholic. A lot of children coming out of a family situation like that usually end up the same way. You didn't."

She got up, tossing the soap back upon the cloth. "I don't know why I'm still punishing myself for having made a mistake in marrying Jean. When I was a child I swore I'd never marry the wrong man like my mom did." Her voice took on a wistful note and she faced Sam. "I had it all figured out. My husband would be loving, giving and sharing. The exact opposite of my dad. Instead I fell for a guy that was interested in using me as a stepping stone to get to the top and I lay right down and let him do it." Her voice quivered. "I'm so angry at myself!"

Sam got up and came over, pulling her into his arms. She didn't resist, resting her head against his chin. "You have a lot of stored-up anger to release, honey. And until you do that, you'll never be free of him or forgive yourself for the mistakes you made." He gave her a small shake. "Dany, don't berate yourself for making errors. The trick is never to repeat the same one twice." He held her at arm's length and offered her a smile. "Just make new ones."

Tears swelled in her eyes and she gave a little laugh. "You're crazy, Sam Reese!"

He leaned down, brushing her lips in a feather-light kiss. "Maybe," he agreed throatily. He raised his head, a lambent gray flame deep in the recesses of his eyes as he studied her for several heart-rending seconds. "You're a very special woman, Dany," he whispered, "and I want the chance to know more about you...your past, your present and what you dream for the future. Just keep trusting me and let's keep talking and both our dreams might get answered if we work at it, honey. Come on, we've got to make some plans for transporting Altair to Santa Barbara." He grinned and pulled her close, giving her a quick hug.

Eleven

———

Dany made a last-minute check on Altair's thickly padded stall that had been specially built within the cargo hold of the airplane. She busied herself with a myriad of details, trying to fight back the fear that shadowed every minute of her day. Where had the two weeks gone in preparation for Santa Barbara? Sam had been with her at least two hours each morning as she took Altair over more complex and demanding jump sequences. She had gained more respect for Sam and his knowledge of the Grand Prix circuit—he was not just an owner of a potential champion, but a man who had valued insight into the demanding world of international jumping events.

Dany made sure the leather cap that Altair wore between his ears was snugly fastened; in case the stallion jerked his head up unexpectedly, the cap could prevent a concussion. Sam had helped her wrap his legs earlier, and she double-checked to make sure that they were holding.

"About ready?" Sam asked, walking up the ramp.

She turned. "Yes."

He smiled, giving the order to remove the ramp. Dany remained at Altair's side as Sam and his ranch hand, Pete, came aboard. Speaking soothingly to the nervous stallion as the door to the aircraft was closed, Dany continued to rub his neck in a reassuring motion. Sam came over, resting against the stall, putting one arm across her shoulders and the other on Altair's shoulder.

"Who's more nervous?" he asked softly. "You or the horse?"

She shook her head. "It's a toss-up," she admitted.

"You'll both do fine, honey."

They landed at Los Angeles International Airport without incident. From there, a horse trailer and truck were waiting to whisk them to the grounds where the Grand Prix event would be held. The temperature was in the nineties, and Dany was thankful for the air conditioning in the truck as they reached their final destination. Her nervousness increased as they received their pass from the gate guard and got directions to the stabling area.

Everywhere she looked she saw sleek thoroughbreds and Hanoverians prancing lightly, eager for workouts. Her pulse picked up more strongly, and a new sense of anticipation spread throughout her. She was proud of Altair and wanted to note the expressions on other riders' faces when she took him out to acclimate him to the grounds. Sam glanced over at her as they pulled into the stabling area.

"You're excited," was all he said, a slight grin shadowing his mouth.

"I shouldn't be. I ought to be scared to death."

He shut off the engine and slid out. "You'll experience both extremes," he warned lightly. "Come on, let's help Pete get this big red horse out of that stuffy trailer before he decides to throw a temper tantrum."

"You want to get him bedded down with Pete and I'll go over to the show office and make sure we're registered with the show secretary?"

"Go ahead," Sam agreed.

People in English riding habits were all about. Their snorting, prancing mounts cantered over the lush grass expanse throughout the complex. As she reached for the screen door, a darkly tanned hand closed over her own.

"*Chérie*, I never expected to see you here."

Dany froze, jerking her hand away. "Jean!" she breathed sharply.

Jean grinned boyishly, taking his riding cap off and bowing gallantly. "The same. Ahh, you look as lovely as ever. And," he murmured, eying her critically, "I would say you are thinner." He grinned broadly, his green eyes dancing with mirth. "You tempt me, Danielle. As always."

Dany's eyes narrowed, and she stepped away from him. "Lying as usual, I see. Save your pretty words to use on someone who cares, Jean." She pulled open the screen, moving quickly inside to the show secretary's desk. Her heart was beating erratically, and anguish coursed through her. Jean had followed her in, and now he stood near the wall, one leg propped lazily over his other booted foot, watching her with amused curiosity.

Her business completed, Dany turned, wanting to run out the door to escape the presence of her ex-husband. She felt his hand on her arm, slowing her down once she was outside.

"Where are you going in such a hurry?"

Dany wrenched her arm away from him, coming to a halt. Her nostrils flared with anger. "Leave me alone, Jean! You've used me and gotten what you've wanted. So quit rubbing salt into the wounds!" she cried.

"Used you?" he echoed, raising his eyebrows. His narrow face became less readable. "Ahh, you think I used you as a stepping stone for success."

"You bet I do."

He shrugged his shoulders eloquently. "But Danielle, it has worked out for you, also. You see, you're riding a Grand Prix candidate yourself. You also benefited from our—liaison. *Oui?*"

Blood was pounding through her skull and she barely held her temper in check. "I'm riding a horse *you* contracted to show! I don't want the limelight, Jean. I never did. Now—" her voice wobbled "—now it's caused so many problems because I have to fulfill the terms of the contract."

Jean frowned. "*Chérie,* you're out of your mind riding that red cow horse. He's got a name on the circuit, you know."

"Which is why you probably left the country," she growled. "This is the first time I've seen you turn tail and be a coward, Jean."

Jean colored fiercely, his dark jade eyes glittering like cold diamonds. "That horse is a killer."

"No more than you are," she hurled back.

He managed a sour grin. "Well, if he doesn't kill you, you'll kill him, *chérie*. Which will it be, eh? Last time it was Crusader's Prince. Who will end up in the hospital this time, I wonder?"

Dany stood frozen, her face devoid of emotion, her heart plummeting to her stomach. Jean had often been short and abrupt during their marriage, but never outwardly cruel. Not like now. Why had he hurled all that old guilt back into her face? She glared at him. "Neither of us," she rasped.

"You're a trainer, not a rider, Danielle." He gave a small bow. "I must be off. I wonder, should I tell the press that two losers are trying to win here, eh?"

She clenched her fist. "You cold-blooded—"

"Listen, when it comes down to my winning this title and anyone threatening my position, I'll make sure I'm not the loser. *Au revoir.*"

Dany purposely walked back to the barn at a slow pace, trying to harness the clashing, roiling emotions that must have been evident on her face. Tears of anger slashed down her cheeks, and she stopped, wiping them away before entering the cool barn complex. Down at the end of the hall in the breezy passageway she could see Sam and Pete saddling up Altair. Compressing her lips into a set line, she took a firmer step, stopping at the tack trunk to grab her hard hat and leather gloves.

Sam smiled down at her as she came around the rear of Altair. Then he frowned, his gaze traveling up and down her rigid body. "Dany?"

"It's nothing," she snapped, taking the reins and leading the stallion out into the paddock. Just as she was about to mount, she felt Sam's restraining hand on her arm.

"Nothing is something," he returned, making it obvious he wanted an explanation.

"Not now, Sam! Give me a boost up on Altair. I need some time to think." She gave him a begging look and he relented. She settled firmly in the Stübben jump saddle, allowing the short stirrups to slide onto her black, booted feet. His hand rested on her knee.

"Warm him up slow, honey," was all he said.

Sam's quiet, reassuring voice assuaged some of the roaring anger, and Dany managed to give a nod of her head. "I will," she promised, her voice thick with tears.

The actual three-mile Grand Prix cross-country course was off limits to the competitors, but a lovely area of two miles of rolling hills with test jumps had been arranged to keep the finely honed athletes in top condition for the performance. It had been nine months since Altair had attended a show, and Dany wanted to check his reactions. The stallion arched his neck, his head perpendicular to the ground as she signaled him to remain on the bit.

Dany worked him in wide circles and figure eights, asking him to switch leads from right to left or vice versa as warm-up. The fields were crowded with some of the finest Grand Prix jumpers in the world, and she purposely shut out their existence, concentrating one hundred percent on Altair's actions and responsiveness. The moment that she took the jump position, her knees and calves firmly against his barrel, body lifted off and slightly forward from the saddle, Altair tensed. The first series of jumps were three-and-a-half to four-and-a-half feet in height, and he scaled them effortlessly.

She worked nearly an hour, finally bringing him down to a slow trot as she came to the gate where

Sam had been standing and watching them. Dropping the reins, Dany slid off the saddle.

"Well?" she asked.

"Honey, you two look like champions out there." Sam pulled the cowboy hat down over his forehead. "Matter of fact, you should have seen every rider on that course watching you at one time or another. They know they have some competition from you two." He grinned and slipped his arm around her shoulders, giving her a hug. "You look good, Dany," he whispered.

Her confidence rose slightly beneath his compliment. She matched his stride, taking off the hard hat and tucking it beneath her arm. As if reading her thoughts, Sam glanced down at her.

"Something's bothering you."

She gave a slight shrug of her shoulders. "I had the misfortune of running into Jean over at the secretary's office," she explained timidly, worried at his reaction. Dany saw his gray eyes turn brittle and probing.

"That's why you were snapping when you mounted up Altair."

"Yes, I'm sorry." They halted at the pickup, and she turned to him. "Oh, Sam, do you really think I have any business showing Altair?"

He gripped her, giving her a small shake. "Every right," he whispered fiercely. "Do you have any idea of how beautiful you and Altair look together as a team? My God, Dany, there wasn't a rider or a trainer who wasn't watching both of you out there earlier. You're championship material." His mouth pulled into an understanding smile. "Come on, let's get over to the motel and get cleaned up. We deserve some rest before tomorrow morning."

She grimaced, climbing into the pickup. "Don't remind me, although the dressage test will be the easiest of the three."

"You'll make them all look easy," he promised, throwing the truck into gear.

Once at the motel, which was a few miles from the show grounds, Sam escorted her to a room which adjoined his own. As if sensing her need to be alone, he left telling her that if she needed anything, to knock on the inner door. In some respects, it was almost like being at home. Dany caught herself wistfully thinking of the ranch as "home," sharply reminding herself that it was only temporary. Pulling off the boots, and stepping out of the breeches and blouse, she took a cooling shower. Wrapped in a towel, she lay down on the bed, falling asleep immediately.

She awoke from the sound sleep near six o'clock that night. Refreshed, Dany slipped into a sleeveless summer dress of pale pink. Funny, she mused while tying the dainty white sash around her waist, I've never wanted to wear dresses before. Sam seemed so appreciative when she did appear in a dress or skirt that his silent admiration coaxed her into rediscovering her femininity.

Knocking softly on the door, she waited patiently until Sam pulled it open. His face mirrored his reaction. "You look lovely," was all he said, but it was enough.

Dany couldn't meet his burning, intense gaze. Each time she was near him, it was agony to stop herself from gliding effortlessly back into his arms. She wanted to rest against the solidness of his body and to be loved openly, without reserve. Memory of that afternoon in the canyon seared her thoughts daily. They had worked so hard in the last two weeks in preparation for Santa Barbara that a stolen kiss or a long embrace was all that had been shared between them.

"With you looking that nice, I'd say we'll have to go someplace special to eat. Hungry?"

"Starved," she admitted.

Sam picked up his Western suit coat, catching her hand and leading her through his room. "Feel better now that you've slept?" he asked.

"Much."

"How's the confidence level holding?"

"It's fragile."

"Mmm, you look incredibly fragile, vulnerable and lovely," he said, turning and gently brushing her cheek with a kiss. He halted at the door and pulled her against him, nuzzling her earlobe with delicious slowness.

Dany moaned softly, falling against the hard oak of his body, hungry for the smell, feel and taste of him once again. He gave her confidence, solace and affection that she was starved for. Turning her head, she felt the molding of his mouth against her parting, yielding lips. It was a searching, hungry kiss, and Sam pulled away, studying her darkly.

"God, how I've missed holding and touching you," he breathed huskily, his breath moist and warm against her face. "Do you know how hard it was not to ask you to stay with me?"

Dany swallowed. "Time, Sam. I needed the time alone," she breathed softly.

His eyes warmed and he smiled, fingers trailing down the length of her clean jawline. "And now, honey?'' he asked lazily, already knowing her answer.

She was afraid to say it. His thumb circled the sensitive skin beneath her earlobe, creating a wild, tingling sensation throughout her whole body. He leaned down, capturing her parted lips in a breath-stealing kiss.

"Say it," he murmured against her lips, brushing them softly. "Say that you want to stay with me tonight, Dany."

Her body quivered beneath his taming fingers, and she sighed languorously, helpless to do anything but surrender. "Yes," she whispered, "I—"

Sam kissed her again, effectively hushing her. He raised his head, cupping her face between his large callused hands. "*Yes* is all I ever need to hear, honey. I need you like I've never needed another woman." His gray eyes darkened with desire as he searched each nuance of her face. "I see the fear in your eyes, Dany. Fear from the past. I won't ask anything more of you until you're ready to give it. Tonight, let me love you like I've dreamed of loving you."

Time eddied and swirled like a slow-moving stream for the rest of the evening. A quiet Chinese restaurant provided the needed tranquility and sense of isolation Dany had sought. She was constantly amazed by Sam's insight into her unspoken requirements, falling more deeply in love with him with each thoughtful gesture he bestowed upon her. As they sat drinking their tea she reflected upon his ability to accurately assess her needs; there was a hidden sensitivity to Sam Reese. Most men with the power of corporations and millions of dollars behind them tended to be shrewd, cold and sometimes even ruthless toward others. She had watched Sam deal courteously with a waiter, the maitre d' and the young man who had parked their vehicle. Yet, when Jean had taken her to dinner, which hadn't been often, he walked with his chin thrust outward, a smugness surrounding him that managed to insult anyone who had to deal with him.

She set her cup down, meeting Sam's melting gray gaze. "You know," she began quietly, "the more I'm around you, the more I wonder what I saw in Jean."

Sam cocked his head attentively, resting his jaw against his folded hands. "Oh? In what way?"

"Little things." She gave a shy smile, embarrassed. "You're so..." She groped for the right words, unused to expressing her emotions or insights. "Why are you so kind to everyone? Jean would embarrass me with his swaggering attitude whenever we went out. You treat everyone as if they were your friend.''

He shared a smile with her. ''Martha beat it into me when I was real young to observe the Golden Rule.''

Dany laughed with him. ''I would think all the money and corporations you own would make you callous.''

''In a lot of owners it does,'' he conceded, toying with the small teacup. ''I learned a long time ago to use brute force or power only when necessary. You get more bees with honey than vinegar, you know.''

Mesmerized by the mellow huskiness in his voice, Dany felt her heart swelling with undeniable love for him. There was a natural agreement of emotions between them, a common ground where both could find solace and protection from the world. The thought of holding him when he felt the need to be cradled against her body sent a new, exhilarating rush throughout her body. She wasn't the only one who needed to be held.

On the way back, Dany persuaded him to make one more check on Altair. Pete met them at the stallion's boxstall. He had arranged a small cot outside the stall door, since no Grand Prix jumper was ever left unattended. Sometimes because of the stress of traveling, time changes or weather conditions, the international athletes would come down with colic. It took the watchful eye of a groom who knew the horse's temperament to be able to spot the first telltale signs of colic, which could kill a horse if the complications were severe enough.

Sam sent Pete on an errand to pick up a few more bales of straw from the main barn, leaving them in the darkness with Altair. Dany allowed the stallion to rest his head against her shoulder as she gently scratched his forelock. Sam remained at her side, his arm around her waist. The night was broken by the softened snort of horses, voices of other grooms further down the dimly lit corridor and the jingle of bits, bridles and saddles being lovingly cleaned one last time before the dawn of the grueling three-day test.

Dany was content to be in the cradle of Sam's arms with Altair nibbling playfully with her fingers, when suddenly the stallion lifted his massive head. Dany looked down the passageway, frowning. A lean figure seemed to melt out of the graying depths, materializing before them like a ghost. She gasped, her eyes widening.

"Jean!"

Her ex-husband stood there, hands languidly resting on his hips.

"Giving your horse a last-minute pep talk?"

Her heart hammered as she heard the steeliness in his softened voice. Simultaneously she felt Sam's arm tighten, bringing her protectively against him. Jean hadn't missed the symbolic and instinctive gesture, and a slow smile tugged at his thin-lipped mouth as he met Sam's hooded gaze.

"I'd think you would be over giving your horse a talk, Daguerre," he returned coolly.

She froze, aware of the brittle truce drawn between the two men who faced one another in the dimness of the passageway. There was no mistaking Sam's warning in his baritone voice, and she saw Jean's eyes flicker with a second of fear. It was such a fleeting reaction that Dany blinked, thinking she had been making it up in her active imagination.

The Frenchman shrugged eloquently, regaining his flamboyant smile. "Monsieur Reese, I can assure you my horse is ready to win handily in every event. I let him sleep."

"Then I suggest you do the same thing."

Dany inhaled softly, her eyes widening. There was nothing compromising about Sam in any way. For the first time she was seeing the dangerous side of his personality. And Jean was fully aware of it, too.

Jean lost his smile, considering the westerner for what seemed an eternity. His eyes flashed with anger, and he swung his gaze to Dany. "Just remember," he breathed angrily, "you'll be alone out there for the next three days. He won't be there. It will be you and me. Remember that."

Sam gently disengaged his arm from Dany, giving her a push toward the truck. "Dany, I'll see you in a few moments."

"But—"

Sam turned his head. "Now," he ordered.

Dany looked at each of them, suddenly shaky with adrenaline. "No, I won't have you fighting—"

Jean laughed. "I only have one question for you, Danielle. Just one."

Sam glared over at him and then back at her as she stood poised like a startled gazelle ready for flight. "Daguerre, I'm warning you—"

She was shaken by the ugly turn of events. Anger soared through her, clearing her confused, muddled thoughts. "What?" she challenged, her voice echoing oddly through the corridor.

Jean pointed to Sam. "Are you allowing yourself to be used again? You're developing a habit of falling in love with men who, shall we say, use your impressive talents with horses.''

His scathing comment sliced into her heart; a knife twisting painfully in her chest. Tears sprang to her eyes, and she covered her mouth with her hands. She heard Sam mutter a curse as he stepped forward, gripping Jean by the collar, slamming him up against the boxstall.

''You son-of-a—''

''No!'' Dany cried.

Sam's grip tightened on the Frenchman until the color drained from his face. Jean struggled, but was no match in size or bulk. Sam growled, ''That's the last filthy thing to come out of your mouth. You hear me?'' His nostrils flared as he glared down at the rider. ''No more insults, Daguerre, or you won't be able to climb up on that horse of yours tomorrow morning. You got that?''

Tears blurred her vision as she stood there watching the two men glare at one another. Finally, Jean gave the barest nod of his head, and Sam released his grip. ''Now get out of here and stay away from Dany,'' he snarled.

He adjusted his shirt, hastily disappearing back into the shadows, his footfalls disappearing quickly, fading into the night. Sam turned, his gray eyes chips of glacial anger as he perused her.

His expression changed swiftly as he saw her standing there in tears. "Dany?"

She took a step away from him, her eyes large and stricken. Was it the truth? Had she fallen in love with Sam just like she had with Jean? Was she making the same mistake again? Oh, God! "No," she cried softly, avoiding his outstretched hand.

"Don't listen to him!" Sam growled. He gripped her arm, halting her flight toward the door of the complex. "Dany, stand still, dammit!"

She whirled around, throwing her hands out, meeting the wall of his chest. "No!" she sobbed, "leave me alone!" All she wanted to do was escape, to have time to think over Jean's horrifying accusation. Was it only a game to Sam? Had he wooed and enticed her all this time just to ride Altair? Her heart shrank in agony against the possibility. But she had done it once, and could do it again. How many times had she heard of women getting a divorce and within a year "bouncing" into another similar situation?

"Honey," he begged roughly, capturing her within his arms and holding her against his body, "it isn't true." He brushed her hair in a kiss, sighing raggedly. "Believe me, Dany, believe . . ."

"I don't know what to believe," she sobbed helplessly, burying her face in her hands.

"Come on," he urged, "we've got some sorting out and talking to do."

It was useless to try and fight him, and she gave in, blinded by her tears, being led like a sobbing child to the truck. By the time they had reached the motel, the tears had ceased. She sat woodenly in a chair within his room as he closed the door. One small lamp chased away the darkness, and his face was shadowed and unreadable as he tossed the cowboy hat and his suit coat to an empty chair. Pulling up another one, he sat opposite her, his face serious and at the same time, probing.

"Let's start from the beginning, Dany," he urged.

"Which one?" she wanted to know, her voice thick and hoarse.

"The one with me. It's the only one that counts now," he countered patiently. "Sure, I wanted you to train and ride Altair. But I would never use your trust or—" His voice softened and there was an unsureness evident in his gray gaze. He stared at her hard for a long moment and finally released a sigh. "This is a hell of a way and time to tell you that I love you," he growled. "I damn near admitted it the day we made love up in the canyon, Dany. But I thought I'd scare you off. I didn't think you were ready for the kind of commitment that I felt toward you." He captured her hands, squeezing them gently. "I wanted to give you the time to work through the anger and hurt of your first marriage, Dany. I was willing to keep our relationship free of any serious commitment until you wanted to take another step."

She stared at him, lips parting, stunned. "You—love me?"

He managed a sour grin. "I suppose it didn't cross your mind that a man from the West might fall in love with a woman from the East?"

Dany gave a shaky laugh. "You really do?" She was like a breathless child in that instant, and Sam groaned softly, getting to his feet, pulling her within the circle of his arms.

"More than life itself, Dany," he whispered roughly, capturing her body solidly against his own, his mouth finding her wet, salty lips.

Time stood on the threshold of eternity in that exquisite moment. A small cry echoed in her throat as she allowed him to deepen the kiss, his tongue finding each sensitive point within her mouth, a molten fire spreading wildly throughout her responding body. He captured her hips against him, and she was aware of his maleness. Entwining her fingers around his thickly corded neck, Dany returned the passion fully, wanting to drown herself completely within him in every possible way.

Dragging his mouth from her bruised lips, he whispered hoarsely, "We belong to each other, Dany. I want to love you so much. These past two weeks have been hell on both of us. Come to bed with me."

She was breathless from his branding kiss, eyes wide and lustrous with invitation. "I didn't know... Oh, Sam, I love you, too. So much that I—"

He bent down, smothering her lips in a soul-searching kiss. "Shh, honey, just show me. That's all I'll ever need...."

If time had halted on the edge of eternity, then infinity was composed of a cocoon of unequaled, shared love. He led her to the bed and with pains-taking slowness, unbuttoned her pale pink dress. She was hypnotized by the tender flame in his gray eyes as he hungrily devoured her upturned face. Slipping his fingers inside the dress, his work-roughened fingers sent thrilling shocks through her body as he slipped it over her shoulders.

Leaning down, he placed light, teasing kisses from her shoulder to her collarbone to the cleav-age of her breasts. Dany drew in a tiny gasp as she felt the bra slipping away from her flesh, being replaced by Sam's tormenting hands. Pushing her gently back against the pillows, he lay down beside her, running his hand across the expanse of her body. Her hair was like a blue black sheet framing her head and shoulders, and Sam smiled, running his fingers through the silken strands.

"You're so beautiful," he whispered against her ear, nibbling at the lobe. Her breathing became shallow and fast as he continued to taunt and tease her until she was arching against him. She waited in a warm, molten haze as he unbuttoned his shirt and undressed fully. Each muscle led cleanly into another, and she stared at him in silent admiration. Welcoming him back to her open arms, Dany sighed softly, closing her eyes, vibrantly aware of his lean maleness.

His mouth closed over her nipple, coaxing it to hardness, and she arched upward, moaning his name over and over again breathlessly, fingers digging deeply into his back. "Please," she cried, "now...please..." Caressing her heated flesh, he stroked the sensitive skin of her thighs, asking entrance to the moist dampness of her yielding body. A fiery hunger seemed to consume her, and she arched to meet him, fusing with him in a primal explosion of volcanic need. Now they were molded into one, the throbbing rhythm sending them to higher and higher levels of exquisite pleasure. Reaching the pinnacle, she froze in ecstasy within his strong embrace, then pressed against his damp body as she felt him tense and shudder, their hearts beating wildly in unison.

A smothering joy enveloped her as she reached out, the flat of her palm against the stubbled roughness of his face. Sam caressed her, taking a deep breath of air. "God, how I love you," he said thickly.

Twelve

Twelve

———

They awoke at exactly six, still clasped in each other's arms. As Dany slowly awoke through the process of bathing and toweling off, it dawned upon her that today was the first of the three tests: dressage. Wrapping the yellow towel around her body, she walked back into the bedroom where Sam was still dozing and began to dress for the event. Climbing into her white breeches and blouse, she felt that she was still wrapped in a blanket of happiness. She was back in the bathroom coaxing her hair into its neat chignon when she saw Sam enter. His hair was tousled and his eyes still filled with sleep as he slid his arms around her waist, drawing her back against him. Dany smiled, closing her eyes, loving his closeness.

"I don't sleep well when you aren't beside me," he breathed against her ear, giving her a kiss on the cheek.

"I could come back to bed, but who will get Altair ready for the dressage test at eight?" she teased, relishing his hard-muscled arms around her.

He raised one eyebrow, lifting his head and staring at her in the mirror. "Good question. Still, I vote for the bed."

Dany turned in his arms, facing him. "You're serious, aren't you?"

Sam rocked her gently back and forth in his arms. "Sure am. It's all your fault, you know. I was going to wait until this show was over to propose to you, lady. I had it all planned. We'd take a couple of days off and go back into the interior. I wanted to woo you with the beauty of the land at its best and then catch you in a mellow moment so that you would be forced to say yes."

She basked in the tenderness of his gaze, reaching up and taming the unruly strands of hair. "Yes to what? I willingly went to bed with you."

He leaned back against the doorframe, cradling her against him. "Is that all you thought I wanted from you? Bed?" he questioned.

Dany caught the seriousness in his eyes and the inflection in his voice. She had been happy and teased him instead of responding to that pensive look dwelling in his pewter gray eyes. A blush swept up her neck and across her face. "Well— I—"

"I told you last night I loved you, Dany. Bed's only a small part of it." He looked around the bathroom, a smile edging his mouth. "This is a hell of a place to propose, you know that?"

She didn't know whether to laugh or cry and stood there resting against his naked body. His smile deepened.

"Well? Will you be my friend, my lover and my wife?"

Tears sprang to her eyes and she opened her mouth and then closed it. He was so right for her; he had been her friend in every sense of the word since their first meeting and it was an ingredient she had sought in her first marriage and found sadly lacking. Sam caressed her cheek, cupping her chin, forcing her to meet his eyes.

"Just nod yes or no," he coaxed.

Dany nodded and Sam picked her up, nearly crushing her in his impulsive embrace. Finally, she gave a half sob and half laugh as he set her back on her feet. He led her from the bathroom and in one deft motion picked her up, carrying her back to his room, depositing her on the bed. She snuggled into his awaiting arms, burying her head against his shoulder, yearning simply to be held, feeling his heart beat like a solid drum against her breast.

"You give me so much happiness," she whispered brokenly.

"Mmm," he growled close to her ear, "it's mutual, honey, believe me."

"I never dreamed . . ." she choked out.

Sam rested above her, absently stroking her bound hair. "What?" he urged.

Dany wiped the tears away. "Oh, my riding master, Terrence," she blurted out softly. She sniffed again. "He always told me to chase the clouds, to go after what I wanted and never be afraid to try it."

"Sounds like a wise old man."

Dany met his warming gaze, melting inwardly. "I loved you from the moment I saw you, Sam, and I was afraid to admit it. Thank God I had the courage to come out West with you."

Sam smiled patiently. "And here we've been fighting like cats and dogs all this time. The instant I saw you it was as if I'd been struck by a bolt of lightning. I was desperate to know you better." He raised his head, frowning. "I think I would have moved heaven and hell to have that privilege, Dany. I knew you were frightened and you were still carrying too many fresh scars from your marriage." He gazed down at her fondly. "Dany, you made my blood run like no woman ever has. Maybe it was your vulnerability, I don't know. You have so much strength of character and I saw it every time you handled Altair, and at the same time, you had the capacity to know when to lean and give in when you were feeling weak."

She gave a small laugh. "I learned a long time ago that pride is the first of my emotions that is expendable. Don't worry, darling, I'll be the first to fall into your arms when I feel like it."

"That's another nice thing about us I like," he murmured, kissing her brow. "We both can say we were wrong and make up. Compromise is so much a part of a successful marriage and I think with one another we have that very rare ingredient."

She nodded, glancing at her watch. "Sam, do you realize in an hour I have to be in the ring?"

He sighed, a quizzical smile pulling at the corner of his mouth. "Spoken like a true horsewoman. You want to leave me for that stallion, is that it?"

She laughed, sitting up on the edge of the bed, straightening out her white blouse. "Give the choice, I'll pick you."

He got up, turning on the shower. "That does my ego a world of good. Give me ten minutes and then we'll get over to the barn area. Pete ought to have him ready to go by the time we get there."

The dressage arena had a solid sand base, making footing for the demanding performance of the three-day eventers excellent. Dany sat quietly on Altair waiting for her number to be called next. A large crowd was watching as horses and riders put themselves through the strenuous, demanding test, politely clapping after each performance. Altair chewed on the snaffle bit, white flecks of foam appearing at the corners of his mouth. Pete patiently wiped his muzzle clean with a damp cloth, patting the horse.

Sam stood at her knee, his hand resting on her thigh. "You're going to knock 'em dead," he said, looking up at her, his mood serious.

She gave a nod. Of the three tests, this was the easiest. The one she dreaded the most was tomorrow morning. "He's ready," she agreed, rubbing the stallion's neck fondly.

"He'll do fine in that snaffle for you," Sam noted. "Tomorrow you'll probably want to switch to the hackamore."

"For the cross-country and the in-stadium jumping," she agreed. It was nearly impossible to have contact with the horse's sensitive mouth without a bit in the dressage portion. Dany said a silent prayer that Altair would continue to bend and flex to her invisible hand movements and do as she asked. Her number, twenty-two, was called and she gathered up the reins. Altair immediately tensed, standing alertly, waiting for the next order.

"Good luck, honey," Sam called, stepping away. He gave her a warm, intimate smile that sent her confidence soaring.

Dressage was the epitome of balance and team-work between horse and human. At the Grand Prix level it was an art; the horse and rider moved together through the intricate steps in a fluid motion. Stopping at the judges' stand, Dany nodded curtly to the three and then swung Altair to one end of the immaculate arena. There was a hushed silence over the crowd. Every fifty to sixty feet a letter was placed along the rail around the oval arena. The rider had to memorize in advance the dressage pattern and at the exact moment the horse paralleled the black and white letter, he was asked to change gait or execute a different delicate, demanding pattern.

Altair flexed beautifully; he was fully on the snaffle, his large nostrils flared, ears back toward his rider and attentive for the signals to come. His copper coat shone like red brass in the early morning sunlight as he broke into a brilliantly extended trot, his long legs thrusting out to their maximum length. It was rare that the dressage crowd would ever whisper or make any noise to break the concentration of horse to rider, but a small ripple of awe passed through the multitude as the stallion's beautifully controlled movements flowed like molten copper into each demanding step.

With the test completed, Dany kept her face straight and serious, bringing Altair back to the center of the arena and once again nodded to the judges, before leaving the ring. She fastened her gaze on Sam in the distance as she rode out at a slow trot, unanimous applause breaking wildly in back of them. Once clear of the crowd, Dany slipped off Altair, giving him an enthusiastic hug. Sam came over, grinning broadly.

"Look at that." He pointed at the scoreboard. "A 72! That's the best score here today. Congratulations." He swept her into his arms, kissing her soundly.

She laughed, returning his hug, stunned by Altair's near-perfect performance. Pete clapped her on the back and, smiling happily, led Altair back to the boxstall while Dany and Sam followed behind at a leisurely pace.

"You don't want to stick around and watch the competition?" Sam asked.

She shook her head. "No, I couldn't stand the tension." She gave him a brilliant smile. "He was wonderful, Sam! What a perfect gentleman!"

He rested his arm across her shoulders drawing her near. "Altair has always come through for me when I really needed him at his best. He's giving you the same now, honey. I think tomorrow will make all the difference in the world. You're going to feel safe on him, Dany."

Her ebullient mood ebbed a bit at the horrifying thought of the cross-country. She resisted the fear that was eating a hole in her confidence, remembering how Altair had saved her life the night of the cattle stampede during the storm. Between Sam's love and Altair's surefootedness, she had little to worry about. Stealing a glance up at Sam's handsome face, she murmured, "Terrence would skin me alive if I didn't ride that wonderful stallion tomorrow. He'd shake his finger, scowl and give me the dickens."

"Well," Sam murmured gruffly, leaning down and kissing her hair, "I think good loving will do the same thing. What do you think?"

She rested against his strong body. "I think you're right, darling."

It was the first day of the rest of her life and Dany knew it. She sat astride the prancing red stallion who snorted with charged vitality as they waited their turn to begin the three-mile cross-country course. Sam had been right: By holding her and loving her all night long he had chased back the fear and put it into proper perspective. She had awakened earlier glorying in the joyous feelings of being loved and loving in return. And it was as if the stallion had sensed her newly found confidence, his flaxen tail lifting and flowing like white silk in the early morning breeze that caressed the demanding course. Today she wore her hard hat, a pair of canary yellow breeches, her black knee-high boots and a white T-shirt with the number twenty-two attached to the front and back of it.

Her mind was zeroed in on the eighteen jumps that would stress and challenge even the most seasoned eventer. Altair hadn't jumped in nine months, and she was aware that he was rusty. She would have to make up the difference. Altair was allowing her to take charge, and he was responsive—something Sam had said he had never done with any of his other riders. She leaned down, rubbing his neck in a soothing circular motion, feeling him relax beneath her gloved hand.

Out of the corner of her eye she saw Jean coming up on his beautiful French thoroughbred. The animal shone like fine steel in the sunlight, moving well beneath Jean's skillful hands.

"Congratulations on your dressage score, *ma chérie*," he greeted, pulling the gelding he rode to a halt.

Dany's eyes narrowed distrustfully. "Not bad for a 'cow horse,' is that it?"

Jean grinned mirthlessly, eyeing the sorrel stallion with a measuring stare. "No, being number two in the standings is not bad at all," he agreed. "Still, that is only one-third of the entire score." His voice dropped, lined with a threat. "You'll be lucky if you don't end up on the ground somewhere on this course today. Did you see that earthen wall? Jump number fourteen? The horses will be tired by the time they reach that devil. I'll bet that half of them won't make the steep angle of it and fall backward.''

"Fourteen is negotiable if you get the proper takeoff point," she said, angry over his suggestion that Altair would not finish the course.

Jean shrugged. "*Oui*. After scaling that monster it is an eight-foot vertical drop on the other side to the water below it. I understand your cow horse hates water. I wonder what he'll do once he sees it? Balk at the top? Rear and sunfish over backward taking you with him?''

She compressed her lips, gathering up the reins to the hackamore. "You aren't scaring me any more, Jean," she warned, her voice cold with fury. "This horse is more surefooted than any other animal here. I'll bet my life on it.''

He smiled thinly. "You may just do that. Anyway, good luck. It's the least I can do for my lovely ex-wife under the circumstances.''

"There's no luck involved, Jean, you ought to know that," she flung back, urging Altair as far away from him as she could get. Anger wove with her confidence, and suddenly, all the butterfly feelings in her stomach ceased. She heard their number being called and trotted Altair up to the chute.

The timer glanced down at his stopwatch, holding a white flag up. Dany swallowed hard, lips flattened, narrowing her perception to the course. The stallion was restive, his small, fine ears flicking back and forth nervously. She glanced to her left, meeting, catching Sam's gaze. In that instant the last of her uncertainty disappeared, and she squeezed the horse's barrel hard with her calves and knees as the buzzer sounded.

Altair lunged forward and the wind sheared at her face making her eyes water from the terrific speed built up within seconds by the thoroughbred. She allowed Altair to stretch to full stride, then she checked him with the hackamore, feeling him immediately slow down his approach to the first fence. She cued him at the exact moment that she wanted him to lift off. The stallion raised his front legs, tucking them high and close to his belly, sailing effortlessly across the four-and-a-half-foot wall which consisted of rough-cut logs. Dany shouted praise in his ear, and she felt a new, strange elation pushing off all of her fears. Just the steadiness of Altair's ground-eating stride was soothing, and her world narrowed to counting off strides, and sizing up the dangerous jumps as they flew along at a dizzying pace.

The first six jumps were warm-ups compared to the next series, and Dany sat deep in the saddle forcing the horse to stretch to his maximum length as the next jump, a triple combination, loomed ahead. Unlike stadium jumps, the cross-country jumps were composed of natural elements for the most part. Logs did not move, stone was solid and earth did not yield. If an eventer hit log, stone or earth, it could end up in a split-second catastrophe.

She heard Altair exhaling great jets of air through his flared nostrils and felt the incredible strength and suppleness of his body moving solidly beneath her as she raised up in the saddle, leaning forward, releasing some of the pressure against the hackamore. The triple combination was composed of earth, logs and brush jammed in between the logs. The stallion launched, his powerful hindquarters propelling them up the slanting combination, forcing him to stretch the full length of his tremendous body. The brush slapped at his legs and belly, and Altair tucked his hind legs deep beneath him as they cleared the obstacle, landing heavily into a pool of muddied water. Snorting loudly, Altair's ears pinned against his neck as he lunged up onto dry land at Dany's coaxing.

Shouts of spectators roared into her conscious-
ness as she swung him sharply up into the thickly
wooded hills toward the most challenging jumps.
She wasn't going to push Altair at a wild, uncon-
trolled gallop just to get the time. He was in magnificent condition and moving easily beneath her
urging. His life wasn't worth a few seconds on the
clock. All she wanted to do was finish the course
in one piece with the horse.

They negotiated twelve and thirteen handily, the
footing becoming slippery because of the morning's heavy dew. There were spectators all along
the course, and as she rounded a steeply inclined
hill, Dany saw television cameras poised near the
fourteenth jump. The seconds seemed like a lifetime as she called to Altair and the stallion at-
tacked the hill. The earthen bank was four feet
above the ground with two logs and a small space
on the top of it. It meant an all-out effort to make
that leap to the bank and then in the next half-
stride, they would have to sail off into space over
the jump that dropped vertically for eight feet into
yet another water hole.

Her hands tightened on the slippery reins. Altair's breathing came in huge enginelike chugs as
he threw himself upward toward the bank. Dany
rose in the saddle, signaling Altair. Clamping her

knees like steel against his barrel, Dany rose perpendicular as the stallion lifted his front end. She literally stood at an angle in the stirrups, body straining over his neck, reins loose so that he could use his neck as a balancing lever. Everything became a blur as the horse sprang like a coiled spring. In a second, they were on top of the bank, clawing at the slippery conditions. Dany felt Altair wobble and threw her weight the opposite direction, giving him his head to rebalance himself. The stallion righted himself and in the same instant was leaping over the poles off the shelf of the bank, airborne, plunging down, his front legs extended like long shock absorbers as they hit the water. The water was belly deep, and Dany fell against Altair's neck, off balance, muddy water surrounding them. Blindly, she gripped his mane, calling him, asking him to go beyond the limits of even his endurance and climb out of the precarious conditions.

Altair lunged out of the water, shaking his head, blowing great jets of moisture from his fully distended nostrils, eyes wide and rolling. He listened to her soothing voice, allowing himself to be directed down the series of small hills toward the flat where the last series of jumps sat.

They came out of the woods, a streak of dark copper flowing against the landscape of greenery. The worst was over and Dany took him safely across the last jumps. Now, only three hundred yards remained to the finish, and she crouched low, like a jockey, pushing him with each flowing stride he took with her hands, legs and body, asking one more second out of his magnificent machine of a body. She was dully aware of the screams, applause and shouts as they raced across the finish line. Dany released the reins, asking him to slow to a canter, to a trot and finally to an exhausted walk. Quickly she slipped off his back, feeling the stallion trembling with the exertion. Worriedly she ran her hands expertly down his legs, concerned that he might have strained a ligament. It was only when Sam placed his hand on her shoulder that she stood up. Both he and Pete were grinning.

"You were magnificent!" Sam said, embracing her.

"Sam, you have the fastest time!" Pete bubbled, taking the stallion and quickly unsaddling him, putting a cooler over his hot, sweaty body.

She collapsed against Sam, so weak that her knees were giving away. He held her against him for a long moment. "You were great out there," he whispered huskily. "Both of you were fantastic. Do you realize the people love you and that red horse of ours?"

Shakily, Sam removed the hard hat, wiping the mud and water from her own face. "We made it, that's all I care about. Oh, Sam, it was a lot harder than I thought," she whispered, closing her eyes and allowing him to support her totally. "Fourteen was the worst jump I've ever encountered. My God, there will be horses killed out there today on that one, Sam. It isn't right," she cried bitterly. "What's the matter with these damn course designers? Can't they tell the difference between a jump that challenges the horse and one that could injure or kill him?"

"Easy, honey, you're coming down out of that adrenaline surge," he soothed softly, guiding her toward the truck that sat in the distance.

Dany wouldn't be consoled. For a long time three-day eventing had been treading a dangerous area: designers were creating jumps that did more than challenge. They were hurting some of the finest jumpers in the world and she wondered when they were going to come to their senses. And fourteen was a murderer. Tears rolled down her cheeks, making white tracks in the grime of her face. Several reporters and photographers ran up to them, begging for a story, and Sam adroitly held them at bay, promising them an interview later after the results were in.

Dany spent half the day rubbing down Altair thoroughly with liniment. There was a camaraderie between Pete and Sam as they worked to make the stallion's tight, tense muscles relax so that he could be rested enough for the in-stadium jumping which would take place tomorrow afternoon. Worriedly, Dany watched as Altair nibbled disinterestedly at his hay. She leaned against the boxstall, just watching him. Sam came over, placing his arm around her waist.

"He's exhausted," he explained. "His appetite will increase by this evening."

"It was a grueling course," she muttered. Looking up into his strong, serene face Dany felt some of her own tension dissipating.

"I don't think either of you were prepared for it, honey. Let's face it, he's been off the circuit for nine months, and this is your first show in four years. Don't be too hard on yourself. You both gave an incredible effort out there this morning. Come on," Sam urged, "let's get you back over to the motel. I think a hot bath and bed are in order for you."

It was dark when she awoke in Sam's room. Dany felt groggy, acutely aware of how many sore muscles were screaming in protest when she moved, sliding her feet across the bed and sitting up. Rubbing her face tiredly, she felt incredibly exhausted. Was Altair feeling the same? He must be, she thought. By the third day, all eventers were incredibly fatigued. They would be no exception to that rule. In-stadium jumping was hard, but not nearly as dangerous as the cross-country portion. She sighed, her dark hair flowing across her shoulders as she bowed her head forward.

"Dany?"

She looked up to see Sam walking quietly from the door of her room to where she sat. "How are you feeling?" he asked, coming and sitting down beside her on the bed.

"Like I've been in an auto accident. Poor Altair, he must be feeling three times as bad as I do."

"Actually I just got done saying good-night to him and he's got his appetite back and eating his way through four quarts of grain right now."

She turned, her eyes widening. "And his legs?"

"Slight puffiness in his rear fetlocks, but nothing more. It's to be expected under the circumstances. Pete's rubbing them down with a good gracing solution right now. He'll be ready to go by noon tomorrow, don't worry.''

She shared a warming smile with him, and leaned over to kiss his strong mouth. Sam groaned softly, slipping his arms around her, laying her back on the bed. His mouth molded tenderly to her lips, parting them, seeking entrance. Finally, he broke contact, his face inches above her own.

''You're beautiful in your sleep, do you know that? I came in to check on you a couple of times and I had to fight the urge to simply lay down beside you and hold you.'' He traced the outline of her eyebrow. ''I'm so proud of you, Dany. You looked like some sort of goddess this morning on Altair, so much a part of him, yet controlling his incredible energy with just a slight, guiding touch of your hand.'' His voice shook with emotion as he drank in every element of her upturned face. ''You are a champion, honey. Never doubt that again. And if you never want to ride again at a show, I'll understand that, too.''

She frowned. ''What do you mean?'' she asked softly.

''I'm not marrying you so that you can ride Altair. I just want you to know that if you decide to quit right now, it would be all right with me.''

A broken smile fled across her lips as she stared up at him. How understanding and sensitive he was! Caressing his jaw, she said, "Sam, as long as I feel capable of doing it, I'm going to continue."

"Why?"

"For the challenge. What else?"

"For me."

She shrugged lightly. "We have a winner. Why shouldn't he be shown to his full potential? You can't help it if your future wife is going to be his rider."

"You're sure about that, Dany?"

She nodded. "Positive."

He pursed his lips, watching her closely. "Well, if he continues to do this well on the circuit, maybe in another year we can retire him to stud and you won't have to show any longer."

Dany smiled provocatively. "Are you going to put me out to pasture, too?" she teased.

"Your choice, lady."

She responded to his hand sliding up the silken material of the dark blue nightgown. Children had been a missing and important ingredient in her life. How many times had she wished for a child? The idea of having children with Sam smothered her with an indefinable joy. Laughing throatily, she pulled him down upon her, kissing him passionately. "I like the idea of children, but I never want to be treated like a broodmare."

He laughed with her. "Somehow, honey, I could never see you having a child once a year for the next twenty or so like a mare does."

"We'll let Altair do his duties and keep the mares happy," she answered, smiling.

Sam turned over on his back, pulling her on top of him. Her black hair fell across her shoulders, framing her oval face as she leaned down, brushing his mouth with a tender kiss. He ran his fingers through the silken mass, his eyes burning with simmering passion. "I'll keep you happy," he growled.

Dany closed her eyes, responding as his hand brushed the fullness of her breast, sighing languidly. "You're one of a kind," she agreed breathlessly. "Just like that red horse of yours."

The day was cloudy and humid with pollution making the sun appear like a dull orange globe in the sky. Dany sat astride Altair, warming him up for the last leg of the three-day event show. Sam had told her that they stood in fourth place among thirty other international competitors last night. At first, she didn't believe him. But then, after a late dinner, he took her over to the secretary's office and gave her a copy of the standings. Altair was showing strongly and to her surprise, had outmatched Jean and his French charge.

Now, the stadium was filled to overflowing with people who loved to watch the very best jumpers in the world compete in a fourteen-fence test of their endurance and strength. By the third day, most eventers were close to exhaustion and only the ones that had been carefully tuned for the grueling pace would be able to make the demanding course with few or little faults. Each time a pole was knocked down, it was considered a fault. If the horse brushed the pole with his front or back feet, it was considered a "tic" but was not counted off as long as the pole remained in its couplings.

The course had to be completed within one hundred fifteen seconds, a little less than two minutes. If the eventer was taken around too slowly, time penalties were given in equivalency of faults. The more faults incurred, the less chance for placing in the top ten for money and trophies. As Dany tested Altair over the warm-up jumps, she saw Jean astride his gray eventer. His time had been two seconds slower than Altair's over the cross-country portion, and she leaned down, stroking her stallion's neck, crooning to him. Altair had courage and heart; it was an unbeatable combination. She was beginning to appreciate his unique upbringing in the Nevada desert, because his footing had been extraordinary under the circumstances yesterday. She knew by listening to several other riders that one horse had to be destroyed because of jump fourteen and that two riders had been sent to the hospital. Altair might be a "cow" horse, but she trusted her life to the magnificent scarred stallion without reserve. He had proven his mettle yesterday to her satisfaction.

Jean rode over, his face set and scowling. "You surprised me, Danielle."

"Oh, in what way?"

"I'd have thought that red devil would be laid up from yesterday's course."

Dany smiled, rubbing Altair's forelock affectionately. "He did well under the circumstances."

"Beginner's luck," Jean drawled.

Anger flared in her eyes. "Luck has nothing to do with it! We've worked long and hard up in the Sierras and it's paying off. What's the matter, haven't you got someone to condition your horse for you now?"

Jean's eyes narrowed. "He'll fall apart on you in there," he warned, ignoring her barb.

"Just make sure your priceless horse doesn't do the same thing. Looks like he's favoring his left front."

He shrugged. "I get paid regardless," was his flippant reply.

Dany glared at him. "Just stay out of our way, Jean, and keep your comments to yourself."

A slow smile pulled at his thin lips. "Yes, you are finally growing into a world-class rider. It looks at though Reese has helped you as much as you have helped his horse."

"Yes, and for once it was done for the right reasons, Jean."

"He loves you?"

"Yes, he does. But not because I will or won't ride his horse. It's not like our arrangement used to be, Jean." Her voice trembled with a backlog of repressed anger and emotion.

He tipped his hard hat in her direction. "My lovely rose is growing thorns. Don't let your standings go to your head, *ma petite*. It's not over yet."

Dany heard their number called, and she gathered up the single reins of the hackamore. She had found that the media had seized upon Altair's background and the fact that he was the only stallion in the competition. Normally eventing was dominated by geldings, a few mares and fewer stallions. The press was also curious to find out why Altair only wore a hackamore, and Dany had twice avoided interviews with reporters, asking Sam to explain the reasons. Many jumpers wore a tie-down or standing martingale so that they could not escape the snaffle bit. Altair wore none, again making him an exception to the rule, creating even more interest.

As she entered the grassy arena, she noted that the jumps were between four feet nine inches and five feet six inches in height. The triple combination, a series of three jumps placed closely together, forced the horse to spread himself across the six feet of the jump. It was not going to be an easy course in any sense of the word. The buzzer sounded and Dany positioned Altair. The moment he leaped over the first jump the timing would begin. She placed him at an angle on the first jump, saving seconds of time that might have been wasted in making a turn to get to the second one. Altair seemed to catch her excitement, his ears laid back, nostrils flared as he thundered down toward a series of three jumps in a row. Dany rated him, asking him to slow up slightly. If he approached the triple jump too quickly, he would miss the all-important midstrides between the second and third jump and would crash into the third one. He sailed cleanly over all three, his legs tucked deeply beneath him on each one.

They scaled two five-foot-three-inch walls composed of poles and painted boards. The water jump was next and Dany urged him up and over that. She glanced back briefly to make sure that he landed well outside the water because if one hoof had landed in the water, it would have been counted as a fault.

Now a series of demanding jumps faced them. She took the double and in an unprecedented move to save time, she pivoted Altair at a gallop on his hind legs on what could only be described as a "roll back" in Western lingo. A roar went up from the crowd as the stallion leaned into the turn pivoting ninety degrees and galloping toward a wall looming eight feet in front of them. Sam shouted encouragement, and she was out of the saddle, leaning over his neck as he pulled out of the jump. They bore down on the two final jumps, taking them handily, and cantered out of the stadium to the wild applause of the cheering spectators. It was a clean round, and Dany grinned, patting Altair on the neck.

Sam and Pete met her near the entrance of the warm-up area, all smiles. Pete simply shook his head. "Mrs. Daguerre, you are one fine rider."

Sam laughed deeply, gripping her hand momentarily. "I don't think any of those English people in there are ever going to recover from the fact that Altair did a roll back in there. That was fantastic, honey!"

She colored beneath his praise. "Thank Altair. If it hadn't been for all his cow-cutting training, I could never have asked it of him."

Sam winked. "Let's cool the old guy out, he deserves it. You have the best time so far."

Pete walked out Altair in the area while they found seats to sit and watch the other contestants. Dany took congratulations from the people around her and anxiously watched as Jean took his French jumper through the course. The horse was obviously favoring his one leg by the end of it, having collected eight faults as a result. Sam kept tabs on the times and faults of the other riders. When the last rider had completed the jumping he turned to her.

"Congratulations, honey. You and Altair took second place. Not bad for a range pony and a beautiful woman who didn't think she had what it took to be the best."

Dany smothered a cry, hand against her lips as she gave him a startled look. She had not entered the competition to win; she had only wanted to come out alive and uninjured. Sam stood, pulling her to her feet.

"Come on, you've got a trophy, ribbon and a sizable check to pick up. Let's get you down to Altair and into the saddle."

As she rode Altair in to receive his rewards the crowd exploded into enthusiastic applause and shouts of encouragement. Tears glittered in her eyes as she accepted the silver bowl and the check. It wasn't a bad day's work for a scarred, abused stallion who had suffered at the hands of more than one rider; but more important she had regained her confidence in her own abilities. Dany leaned down with her head against Altair's arched neck, hugging him without reserve. She sat back up, and waved to the crowd as she took a victory canter around the arena. As they rode out of the arches she saw Sam waiting for them in the distance. She and Altair were both riding toward a future that was paved with happiness and a shared commitment. If it hadn't been for Sam, she might have never restored her confidence.

Halting Altair, Sam dismounted, handing the trophy and reins of the stallion to Pete. She didn't care if the eyes of the entire world were watching them as she walked up to him. A lump wedged in her throat, effectively silencing her.

"Come here," Sam commanded softly, opening his arms to her.

With a tearful smile she stepped inside the circle of his arms. He embraced her tightly, for a long time, his head resting against her own. Sam made it easy for her to lean on him when she wanted. The thought flooded her heart with love, and Dany embraced him fiercely in return.

He pulled scant inches away, his eyes strangely moist. Dany reached up and caressed his leathery cheek. "We can't stand out here like a couple of children crying," she muttered, dashing her tears on her own cheek away with the back of her hand.

He smiled tenderly, leaning over and brushing her waiting lips in a kiss. "Why not?" he demanded gruffly, pulling her close. "They're tears of joy."

Dany closed her eyes, content to remain against his incredibly strong body. "I don't mind crying for happiness," she admitted.

"Then we'll be crying often, honey."

Dany smiled blissfully. "We owe you so much, Sam...."

"Shh," he commanded, placing a kiss on her hair. "There is no scorekeeping where we're concerned, Dany. Never." He tucked her beneath his arm, leading her away from the stadium.

Dany stole a look up at him as they walked toward the quieter area of the stables. There was an unspoken aura of happiness lingering in his lightened gray eyes. He walked like a man who was on top of the clouds. She was there, too, she realized. "You've helped me chase the clouds, Sam," she said, catching his gaze.

His hand tightened momentarily against her waist. "Your riding master taught you that, didn't he?"

"Yes. But thanks to you, I was able to scale a few hurdles of my own to reach those heights."

Sam tried to appear nonchalant about his part in the healing of her fears. "I don't know, honey," he drawled, "when you've got a hammerhead of a stallion and a stubborn cowboy from California to help, how can you lose?"

Dany laughed fully, reaching up impulsively, curving her arms around his neck. Sam drew to a halt, a careless smile edging his mouth. "More than that," she whispered, "I've fallen in love. And that means more than scaling the heights of any career." Her voice shook with emotion. "More than anything," she promised fiercely.

He lost his smile, studying her in the intervening silence. "We've all found love in one another, honey. And when you've got love like we do, everything else around us automatically turns to success."

"I'll never care about the trappings of success, Sam. All I'll ever need is your love and understanding," she admitted softly.

He groaned, sweeping her against him. "And you've had my love since the day we met," he murmured thickly. "You're mine, now and forever."

* * * * *

Harlequin Romance ®

Delightful

Affectionate

Romantic

Emotional

Tender

Original

Daring

Riveting

Enchanting

Adventurous

Moving

Harlequin Romance—the
series that has it all!

HROM-G

HARLEQUIN PRESENTS®

HARLEQUIN PRESENTS
men you won't be able to resist falling in love with...

HARLEQUIN PRESENTS
women who have feelings just like your own...

HARLEQUIN PRESENTS
powerful passion in exotic international settings...

HARLEQUIN PRESENTS
intense, dramatic stories that will keep you turning
to the very last page...

HARLEQUIN PRESENTS
The world's bestselling romance series!

PRES-G

◈ *Harlequin*® ◈ *Historical*

If you're a serious fan of historical romance,
then you're in luck!

Harlequin Historicals brings you
stories by bestselling authors, rising new stars
and talented first-timers.

Ruth Langan & Theresa Michaels
Mary McBride & Cheryl St. John
Margaret Moore & Merline Lovelace
Julie Tetel & Nina Beaumont
Susan Amarillas & Ana Seymour
Deborah Simmons & Linda Castle
Cassandra Austin & Emily French
Miranda Jarrett & Suzanne Barclay
DeLoras Scott & Laurie Grant...

You'll never run out of favorites.

Harlequin Historicals...they're too good to miss!

HH-GEN

THAT'S INTRIGUE—DYNAMIC ROMANCE AT ITS BEST!

Harlequin Intrigue is now bringing you more—more men and mystery, more desire and danger. If you've been looking for thrilling tales of contemporary passion and sensuous love stories with taut, edge-of-the-seat suspense—then you'll *love* Harlequin Intrigue!

Every month, you'll meet four new heroes who are guaranteed to make your spine tingle and your pulse pound. With them you'll enter into the exciting world of Harlequin Intrigue—where your life is on the line and so is your heart!

Harlequin Intrigue—we'll leave you breathless!

INT-GEN

LOOK FOR OUR FOUR FABULOUS MEN!

Each month some of today's bestselling authors bring
four new fabulous men to Harlequin American Romance.
Whether they're rebel ranchers, millionaire power brokers
or sexy single dads, they're all gallant princes—and
they're all ready to sweep you into lighthearted fantasies
and contemporary fairy tales where anything is possible
and where all your dreams come true!

You don't even have to make a wish...Harlequin American
Romance will grant your every desire!

Look for Harlequin American Romance wherever Harlequin
books are sold!

HAR-GEN

He'd blown back into town like a

DUST
DEVIL

REBECCA
BRANDEWYNE

She was young and beautiful; he was the town's "Bad Boy." They shared one night of passion that turned Sarah Kincaid into a woman—and a mother. Yet Renzo Cassavettes never knew he had a child, because when blame for a murder fell on his shoulders, he vanished into thin air. Now Renzo is back, but his return sets off an explosive chain of events. Once again, there is a killer on the loose.

Is the man Sarah loves a cold-blooded murderer playing some diabolical game—or is he the only port in a seething storm of deception and desire?

Find out this March at your favorite retail outlet.

MIRA The brightest star in women's fiction

MRBDD

To an elusive stalker, Dana Kirk is

FAIR GAME

JANICE KAISER

Dana Kirk is a very rich, very successful woman. And she
did it all by herself.

But when someone starts threatening the life that she has
made for herself and her daughter, Dana might just have
to swallow her pride and ask a man for help. Even if it's
Mitchell Cross—a man who has made a practice of
avoiding rich women. But to Mitch, Dana is different,
because she needs him to stay alive.

Available at your favorite retail outlet this March.

MIRA The brightest star in women's fiction

MJKFG

This April, find out how three unsuspecting
couples find themselves caught in the

The Parent Trap

Sometimes love is a package deal....

Three complete stories by some of your
favorite authors—all in one special collection!

DONOVAN'S PROMISE by Dallas Schulze
MILLION DOLLAR BABY by Lisa Jackson
HIS CHARIOT AWAITS by Kasey Michaels

Available this April wherever books are sold.

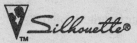

SREQ496